ONLY ONCE

(A Sadie Price FBI Suspense Thriller—Book 4)

Rylie Dark

Rylie Dark

Debut author Rylie Dark is author of the SADIE PRICE FBI SUSPENSE THRILLER series, comprising six books (and counting); the MIA NORTH FBI SUSPENSE THRILLER series, comprising six books (and counting); the CARLY SEE FBI SUSPENSE THRILLER, comprising six books (and counting); and the MORGAN STARK FBI SUSPENSE THRILLER, comprising three books (and counting).

An avid reader and lifelong fan of the mystery and thriller genres, Rylie loves to hear from you, so please feel free to visit www.ryliedark.com to learn more and stay in touch.

BOOKS BY RYLIE DARK

SADIE PRICE FBI SUSPENSE THRILLER
ONLY MURDER (Book #1)
ONLY RAGE (Book #2)
ONLY HIS (Book #3)
ONLY ONCE (Book #4)
ONLY SPITE (Book #5)
ONLY MADNESS (Book #6)

MIA NORTH FBI SUSPENSE THRILLER
SEE HER RUN (Book #1)
SEE HER HIDE (Book #2)
SEE HER SCREAM (Book #3)
SEE HER VANISH (Book #4)
SEE HER GONE (Book #5)
SEE HER DEAD (Book #6)

CARLY SEE FBI SUSPENSE THRILLER
NO WAY OUT (Book #1)
NO WAY BACK (Book #2)
NO WAY HOME (Book #3)
NO WAY LEFT (Book #4)
NO WAY UP (Book #5)
NO WAY TO DIE (Book #6)

MORGAN STARK FBI SUSPENSE THRILLER
TOO LATE (Book #1)
TOO CLOSE (Book #2)
TOO FAR GONE (Book #3)

CHAPTER ONE

The wind sounded like a mad thing, the howling seeming to fill every inch of spare space on the rig, creeping round corners and then hurtling down the stairs into the bunks. Accompanied by the crashing of the waves on the Beaufort Sea coastline in the dark north of Alaska, the sound was almost demonic. It was enough to give the derrick hands nightmares, at least while they were still new, before they got used to it and it became nothing more than background noise.

Paul Montford was used to it. He had been here a long time. He lay awake, staring at the top of his bunk, listening to Russ on the bed above him, snoring loudly. Now that was a sound that could regularly keep him awake.

The siren sounded, waking them up for morning rousting. Time to get up. Russ's snoring stopped abruptly. His legs and torso appeared in Paul's eyeline as he jumped down from the upper bunk.

"You awake, man?"

"I've been listening to you snore for about an hour. You sound like a goddamn bear," Paul complained as he sat up. Russ just chuckled.

They dressed hurriedly in the half-light, packing on twenty pounds of gear to insulate against the freezing conditions outside. Worse than freezing; it could go as low as minus twenty-eight degrees Fahrenheit on some days. Inside the berth, the lights were dim, perhaps intentionally so that the perpetual darkness outside was not so much of a shock. Even in the summer months, light was precious. Right now, it was perpetual gloom, but after ten years working the rig, Paul was used to it. He couldn't imagine doing anything else. His fellow derrick hands were like his family.

Not that everyone could cope with it. Suicides happened. The occasional polar bear attack on the ice floats. Rumors of men going mad in the dark and the cold.

Paul just got on with it. Life was a predictable round of drilling, eating, and sleeping. There wasn't much time for anything else. That predictability, the routine and the sense of being buffered from the outside world, made him feel as though he was safe here.

1

A lot of derrick hands were running from something. There was a joke that if Alaska was a place that people fled to, then the rigs were the place to flee from Alaska.

There was nowhere to go from here; they were literally at the ends of the earth.

Paul followed Russ up the steps toward the higher decks to reach the small dining hall. His stomach growled loudly.

"Now who sounds like a bear," Russ joked.

"Shut up," Paul rejoined, good-naturedly.

Even with the twenty-pound gear, the early morning cold hit him as soon as he stepped onto the higher decks. All around, the gray waves roiled and crashed against the backdrop of an inky sky. Paul thought it looked beautiful, in an eerie, wild kind of way.

Others, he knew, would think that this was hell on earth. He had to brace himself against the wind, which could sustain speeds of thirty miles per hour. It whipped against him, and he took a deep breath and squinted against the gloom.

Then something caught his eye. Hanging above him, being whipped around in a frenzy by the driving wind, it took Paul a few moments to realize what he was looking at.

It was only when he felt Russ tense up next to him and heard the low groan that came from his colleague's mouth that he processed the sight of the body hanging from the flare boom crane, sixty feet above him.

His first thought was that someone had had enough. One of the newbies, driven to despair by the harsh conditions and the past two months of perpetual darkness.

But then someone shone a flashlight on the swinging body and caught the man's face full on before the wind whipped it out of sight again. It was just a few seconds, but it was long enough for Paul to see the man's expression, and he knew that face was going to haunt his dreams.

It was frozen in an expression of sheer terror, and Paul suddenly felt very, very certain this was no suicide.

It was murder.

CHAPTER TWO

Sadie Price, star of the FBI Behavioral Analysis Unit, sat outside the inner office of her senior agent, ASAC Paul Golightly, and tried not to vomit all over the pale green carpet.

She felt sick with worry, even though if anyone had studied her face, she would seem perfectly calm. She had put on her best pant suit over her thermals and under her fur-lined winter parka, and wrestled her unmanageable hair into submission, pinning it back into a neat bun. She needed to look unflappable, like someone who had nothing to worry about at all.

Like someone who wasn't guilty.

The original date for the hearing had been postponed while Sadie had been wrapped up in a tough case, and she had been able to put it at least partly out of her mind until the Internal Affairs investigators at Quantico had suddenly decided that, as Sadie's new posting to Anchorage, Alaska, had turned out to be a lot busier than anyone could have expected, they would come to her.

She wondered if she was expected to thank them for the convenience.

It had always been going to happen, she knew, but now that it was here the possible consequences were beginning to take shape in front of her, threatening her with the potential of becoming reality. If it was decided that she had been less than honest in her account of the killing of the Gestalt Mangler, then she could lose her badge.

Worse, she could find herself accused of murder.

It was unlikely that it would ever go that far. Sadie was a national hero, credited with bringing down some of the worst killers in recent years. The Gestalt Mangler, as the press had dubbed him, had been her most high-profile case and the media pundits might have expected a medal rather than an investigation into Sadie herself. Right now, it was all being conducted very discreetly, but that could change.

She could only hope that the powers that be at Quantico, the FBI headquarters, weren't about to throw their star investigator under the bus. She knew that her sudden request to be transferred to Alaska, at a

3

time when her star was rising exponentially, could seem suspicious, as though she was running away from her own guilt.

Running away from the ghosts of the present straight back into the arms of the ghosts of the past. Sadie had been born and raised in Alaska, in the hinterlands on the outskirts of Anchorage, assuming that you could call her father's often violent and neglectful parenting style in any way being "raised." Nurturing, it was not.

But she had her reasons for returning, her sister's still unsolved death being the main one.

There was no time to think about that now. Agent O'Hara, the Anchorage Field Office's newest and youngest recruit, came into the outer office and smiled nervously at her.

"They're ready for you, Agent Price."

"Thanks." Sadie stood up, took a deep breath, and walked into the room. O'Hara shut the door behind her, leaving them. He was too much of a rookie to be privy to an Internal Affairs investigation with a special agent of Sadie's standing.

Golightly was there, though, sitting at the conference table with three Internal Affairs investigators. The stenographer was in the corner, ready to record her every word. Sadie swallowed and her throat felt like sandpaper.

As she greeted the investigators and took her seat, she scanned them quickly, not recognizing any of their faces. One was a woman in her fifties, with a gray bob that looked like a helmet and eyes that were just as hard. Of the men, it was obvious that Quantico had sent their finest, most polished-looking agents with chiseled jaws and an air of cold professionality. The youngest of them was pushing thirty, Sadie's age, and looked as though he may be just a little more sympathetic than the woman and the older man. There was a little warmth behind his eyes at least.

"Agent Price. Shall we begin?" It was the woman, who had introduced herself as Special Agent Lawson, who began, her voice clipped and cool. There would be no emotion in the room, Sadie knew. Internal Affairs investigations were detail driven. Trying to defend her actions with a plea to the obvious terror of being cornered by one of the most sadistic serial killers in history wasn't going to help her.

She took a slow breath, her expression carefully neutral. Reminding herself to stick to her story. That she had done nothing wrong.

The Gestalt Mangler had deserved to die.

4

"It has come to our attention that there are discrepancies between your account of events on the night in question and the autopsy report on the body of Henry Aspen. You have of course been made aware of this," Lawson began, looking down at the statement in front of her. She was clearly the lead on the investigation, but Sadie doubted she would be any easier on her simply because she was another female.

It was hard to think of the Mangler as Henry Aspen. It was such a normal, middle-of-the-road name for a man who had been nothing short of a monster. There was no one who was going to mourn him.

Nevertheless, the law was the law, and it was Sadie's job to uphold it, not to take it into her own hands.

"Yes," Sadie acknowledged the woman's statement. What she wasn't aware of was the nature of the discrepancies, although she was pretty sure she could guess.

Lawson wasted no time in getting straight to the point.

"Firstly, in your original statement you say that Aspen had you cornered, and that in your initial altercation your gun had been kicked out of your reach."

"Yes," Sadie said again, trying not to remember the panic that she had felt at being potentially at the Mangler's mercy. The terror of ending up like his victims, with their bodies unrecognizable after a terrifying, tortured death.

"Agent Price," the younger of the men, Special Agent Seymour, cut in, "can you please take us through your account of the night in question?"

Sadie pressed her lips together, feeling nauseous again. It wasn't a night that she wanted to relive. In spite of the cold inside and out, she felt herself beginning to sweat.

Nevertheless, her voice was calm as she recounted her statement, even as the memories assailed her.

The Mangler's rancid breath in her face as he almost panted with excitement at the thought of her, his hunter, now becoming his prey. The sense of futility as she had realized that she couldn't overpower him. Sadie wasn't used to feeling powerless, not since she had been a little girl at the mercy of the whims of her father.

He's going to torture me. The thought had occurred to her with astonishing clarity. He was going to torture her, and then she was going to die. And her whole life would have meant nothing.

5

Then her grasping fingers had found something hard...and she heard the sound of flesh crunching as she hit Aspen with all her strength...

"This is where the discrepancy comes in, Agent Price," Lawson said, her cool tone slicing through Sadie's memories. "You say that you hit Aspen in the head with the chunk of rebar once. Yet according to our autopsy report, there is indication that there may have been more than one blow. Perhaps even a succession of them." Lawson's voice was accusing, but Sadie heard the word "may" and felt some relief. That one word meant that they didn't feel certain. It was a maybe.

"Yes, I did," Sadie reaffirmed. "I hit Aspen with the rebar once, in the head."

Almost imperceptibly, Lawson raised an eyebrow.

She didn't believe her, Sadie could tell.

"You are absolutely certain of that?"

Sadie met the woman's gaze head on. "Yes," she said.

In the corner of the room, the stenographer's hands moved furiously, recording every word.

"Very well. However, there is also another, perhaps more concerning, discrepancy," Lawson continued. Sadie held her breath and said nothing, waiting for the woman to continue.

"The coroner is certain that the rebar killed Aspen, due to the force of the blows..."

"Blow," Sadie corrected, her voice rising a little in annoyance.

"According to you, blow," Lawson amended. "Aspen died due to the force of the blow to the head. And yet, you still shot him."

"I did shoot him. Once," Sadie confirmed. "I hit him with the rebar, then grabbed for my gun and shot him before he could come at me again. He was armed. He had made his intentions towards me known." Her voice wavered a little on the last words and she mentally tried to steel herself against what was now a physical memory of her fear and disgust.

She felt Golightly's gaze on her, and her eyes flickered toward him. There was sympathy there. Golightly had been impressed with her when she had solved a trio of complex cases after her return to Alaska. She also suspected that the gruff native Alaskan would be thoroughly of the mindset that a little rough justice wasn't always a bad thing, and the world was a better place without the Mangler.

"That's also what your statement says," Lawson went on, "but if it was the blow—or blows—that killed him, then he was no longer on the attack. There was no need for you to shoot him. It seems like overkill, Agent Price."

She sounded more like a prosecutor than an Internal Affairs investigator with that comment, Sadie thought, feeling a flare of anger. *Overkill, Agent Price.*

She remembered her finger around the trigger, the calm certainty as she had stood and watched him dying that she had done the right thing.

"In the moment, I had no way of knowing that the blow had killed him," Sadie argued, aware that she sounded defensive and that her voice was beginning to rise. It wouldn't help her. "It all happened in a matter of seconds. I hit him, dropped the rebar, grabbed for my gun, and shot him. It was self-defense."

Lawson went to speak but Seymour cut in. "You believe that you were acting in self-defense," he said, and Sadie wasn't sure if he was correcting her or validating her. Sadie looked into his eyes and was sure that she saw sympathy there too.

"Yes," she said, "I do. I acted in fear for my life."

Only Lawson looked unconvinced, and Sadie had the sinking feeling that it was going to Lawson's judgment that carried weight.

There was a brief silence, and then a sudden knock at the door made Sadie jump in her seat.

It was Agent O'Hara. Golightly glared at him for interrupting.

"What is so important, Agent, that it couldn't wait?"

O'Hara's eyes swept around the room. He looked nervous. "It's delicate, sir."

Golightly got up and left the room. Sadie could hear them outside the door, speaking in hushed tones. She saw Lawson pressing her lips together as though angry at the interruption and suppressed a smile. This wouldn't have happened down at Quantico, but this wasn't Quantico; this was Alaska.

Golightly walked back into the room looking grim and Sadie felt herself tense. Something had happened. A new case? She felt a surge of adrenaline. She wanted to be back out there, not stuck in a stuffy room around a conference table.

"Agent Price? A word." Golightly jerked his head toward the door. As Sadie stood up, Lawson looked from her to Golightly, her face angry.

"We are in the middle of an investigation," she said.

"I apologize, but this is important," Golightly said, holding the door open for Sadie. She excused herself and walked out of the room, turning to Golightly as the door shut behind him.

"Sir?"

"There's been a call come in from one of the rigs up on the Beaufort coastline," he said without preamble. Golightly rarely used more words than were necessary. "A murder."

Sadie frowned. This didn't sound anywhere near important enough for the ASAC to interrupt an important investigation.

Then she thought about the location. The Beaufort Sea was part of the Arctic Ocean, one of the least explored oceans in the world. Its coastline was a freezing, frigid place, more ice than land, at the northernmost part of the state. She had never been there, because it just wasn't the sort of place anyone ever went to for a vacation.

As a result, it was unclaimed by any local police division, which meant that the murder would of necessity be passed to FBI.

"You want me to go and investigate," she said. A statement, not a question. Golightly nodded, and Sadie shook her head.

"With respect, sir," she said, trying not to show how pissed she felt, "any agent could take this on, surely? This investigation isn't going away, and Lawson in there is already out for my blood. I can't interrupt the investigation just to take a new case on."

"I decide that, Agent Price," Golightly said, although without any sign of anger at her refusal. "All of my best agents are still tied up on the child pornography case that you uncovered over Christmas."

"Agent O'Hara isn't," Sadie argued. She glanced at the door as though she could see through it, imagining the three Internal Affairs investigators getting more and more impatient. It was hardly going to endear her to them. "He needs to get his teeth into something. He's still a rookie."

"I'm sending him," Golightly agreed, "but this could be sensitive. I don't want a wet behind the ears new agent heading this up. Sure, I could pull one of the other agents off the kiddie case, but I want my best agent on this. That would be you."

Sadie dipped her head with a slight smile, acknowledging the praise. Even so, she didn't understand the rush.

Preempting her next question, Golightly said, "I've sent O'Hara to get you a flight. You will need to leave soon. As soon as you can, in fact. I'll let the investigators know."

Sadie hesitated. The last thing she wanted to do was give Lawson any more reason to distrust her. She wasn't enamored of the idea of repeating the last half hour either.

"Don't worry about the guys from Quantico," Golightly assured her. "I'll let them know it isn't your fault. That I'm insisting you go because you're my best agent. That can hardly go against you."

"Thank you," Sadie said, and then hesitated. "What makes it sensitive?" she asked, wondering for a moment if Golightly was just trying to get her out of the investigation.

"The body—one of the derrick hands—was found hanging from a crane on one of the platforms."

Sadie frowned. "Okay. How do we know it wasn't a suicide?" It was far from unheard of. Being a derrick hand on a rig was backbreaking, lonely work, and the Beaufort Sea was a desolate place.

"HIs hands were tied behind his back."

She exhaled slowly. "Okay, that will do it. But I still don't understand, what makes it sensitive? What are you not telling me?"

"I know as much as you, Agent Price," he said, raising a bushy eyebrow. "But what do you think? You're the brains."

Sadie smiled tightly. She was already there.

This wasn't the result of some kind of argument between the derrick hands, or someone with a personal grudge. No one hung a body from a crane unless they were trying to send a clear message.

This wasn't just a murder.

It was an execution.

CHAPTER THREE

Sadie walked through the Anchorage Field Office with Agent O'Hara eagerly in step beside her. O'Hara had been a little starstruck by her ever since she had arrived, and he currently had a look on his face that reminded her of an excited puppy. She hoped he managed to get over it before they reached the murder scene, because she needed him clear and focused, not following her around like a lost love.

Although she liked O'Hara, Sadie had always preferred to work a case alone, or at least as much as was possible without putting herself in serious danger or jeopardizing the case itself. When she was immersed in a murder investigation, she found that she was ultra-focused, and wanted to be free of the distractions of others. When she had put in a transfer to return to her home state of Alaska—a move that many saw as a step backwards in her career—she had expected that she would get more chances to do just that. The Anchorage Field Office covered a huge jurisdiction and had fewer agents than other offices.

Yet since she had been back, she had been partnered on nearly every case with the local sheriff, Logan Cooper, and sometimes the deputy too, his sister, Jane. Local cops were usually the worst partners for an FBI agent, in her experience, because they inevitable saw the Feds as interfering in their local area and trying to take over.

The Coopers had been no exception. At least at first.

After a dangerous murder case had used all of their combined resources, they had become friends. Sadie was often amazed by how well she worked with the sheriff.

Sometimes, she thought they worked together a little too well.

She felt heat rise to her face as she thought of their conversation a few weeks ago on Caz's porch. Cooper had pretty much asked her for a date, but she had never had the chance to respond. Instead, she had been called to her dying father's bedside.

He hadn't mentioned it since, and as she had been based back at the field office, she had barely seen him, except when he came into the saloon with Jane. The saloon was owned by Caz, who was another new friend and now Sadie's landlord, a tattooed, butch woman with a tough exterior and a soft heart. She was a single mom to a little girl named Jenny, whom Sadie had a large soft spot for.

Sadie had come to Alaska looking for some kind of redemption and had ended up finding a home.

The closure she needed still eluded her, though. Her estranged father had been the only one who could tell her anything about her sister's death, and who might have information that could help her solve what Sadie knew in her heart was a murder.

But he had died before he could tell her anything, instead leaving only a crudely drawn map that was proving hard to decipher. Sadie had given up on it and passed it to Cooper to work on a week before.

She realized that she wasn't going to get the chance to say goodbye before she flew off to the north. They were leaving to go to the helipad now.

"What do you think?" O'Hara asked, cutting through her thoughts. He was in his mid-twenties, half a decade younger than Sadie, but she thought he looked younger. Or perhaps it was just that he didn't yet have that jaded look that all agents got sooner or later, especially if they were working big cases.

Murders, drugs, trafficking. All the good stuff, Sadie thought wryly.

She deliberately avoided thinking about the Mangler again.

"Difficult to say until we get there," Sadie told him. "There's very little to go on at the minute. Once we know exactly how the derrick hand was killed, and how the hell he got up on that crane, we might have something to go on."

"Golightly thinks it isn't going to be straightforward."

"They rarely are," Sadie said with a sigh. As much as she could feel her adrenaline rising at the prospect of a new case, the thought of the desolate location unnerved her a little. Anything could happen to the men on the rig, really, and who would ever know?

Suddenly, she was glad she wasn't going alone.

They reached the entrance doors and Sadie stepped outside into a burst of bright sunshine that made her blink rapidly. At this time of year, they only had a few hours of sunlight a day, but right now the sky was clear and dazzling, the sun sparkling off the snow on the ground like it was crystal.

Momentarily blinded by the cold light, she didn't realize who had stepped in front of her.

11

"Price. I was hoping to catch you. I needed to bring some documents over to the agent heading up the local child pornography case."

Sheriff Cooper. Seeing him silhouetted by the sun and dressed in dark jeans and a buckskin coat with his sheriff's badge pinned conspicuously to the front, his green eyes twinkling against tanned skin, Sadie felt caught off guard.

"Cooper," she said, watching his full lips curve into a devastating smile. The sheriff was one of those rare men who genuinely didn't realize just how good-looking he was. "You couldn't use e-mail like everyone else?"

He shrugged, grinning. "You know what the internet signal is like back at the station. We don't get the funding that you guys do. We're on a shoestring budget over there."

Sadie rolled her eyes but grinned back. Bantering with Cooper made her feel calmer and grounded back down to earth after what had so far been a heavy morning.

"Get over it, Sheriff. This is Agent O'Hara, by the way. O'Hara, Sheriff Cooper. We're on our way to the rigs out on the Beaufort coastline."

Sheriff Cooper raised an intrigued eyebrow, but knew better than to ask, at least in front of O'Hara, who was looking from Sadie to Cooper with a slightly puzzled expression. He also looked, she thought, disappointed.

Sadie hoped the young agent didn't have some kind of crush on her. That was going to be awkward.

"Do you know how long you'll be gone?" The sheriff kept his tone light, but Sadie heard—or hoped she did—a tinge of disappointment that mirrored O'Hara's expression.

"No idea. Hopefully it will be a cut and dried case."

"Because you have such a great track record with those," Cooper said, only half joking. The bright sunlight seemed to suddenly dull as Sadie thought of the last case they had worked together. It should have been enough to put her off men altogether. It had certainly left her questioning her own judgment, and at the same time her father's death had brought up a maelstrom of long buried emotions that she was still struggling to process. It wasn't a surprise that Cooper hadn't raised the question of a date since.

She was glad he hadn't. Wasn't she?

"Well, there's always a first time," she said lightly.

12

Cooper nodded, then sensing her mood he changed the subject. "I was hoping to catch you, so it's just as well I did come over. How did the investigation go?"

Sadie hesitated and looked over at Agent O'Hara, who coughed awkwardly. "I'll go and wait for you over the road, Agent Price. Nice to meet you, Sheriff Cooper."

Cooper watched him go, looking amused. "Fresh out of Quantico?"

"A year, I think. This could be his first big case. The Internal Affairs investigation was cut short by the call coming in from the rig, but I couldn't call it." Sadie shook her head. "I feel like there should be every reason not to worry, but I'm also sure that the lead investigator wants to hang me out to dry."

"So, you have to do it all over again?" Cooper looked sympathetic.

"I already told them all I could, but I've got a feeling they'll make me repeat it anyway," she said with a sigh. Although at first, she had been glad of the interruption, now she realized she could be just prolonging the inevitable.

The end of her career. Possibly even jail time. She shuddered at the thought and pushed it hurriedly to the back of her mind. Right now, there were other things that needed her attention.

The main one was hanging somewhere over the Beaufort Sea.

"I was working on your father's map last night," Cooper said. "I think I might know where it starts. Hopefully by the time you get back, I can be sure."

Sadie met his eyes and saw the warmth in them. "Thank you," she said, meaning it. Her sister's death was a reopened cold case now, thanks to the sheriff, and something that they were both working on together. His opening up the files had given them the lead that had led to her father drawing this map.

If they could just decipher what was essentially a page of squiggles, it might just lead them somewhere.

"I had better go," she said, although part of her didn't want to go anywhere. "See you, Logan."

She didn't use his first name often, and she saw a flicker of surprise in his eyes that turned into pleasure. They stared at each other, and something passed between them, until Sadie dropped her eyes and Cooper gave an embarrassed cough. The moment—whatever it had been—was over.

"Call me if you need me," he said. "I mean, I know you rely on me to solve your cases."

13

"You wish," she said, grinning, and then jogged over to the road toward O'Hara, raising her hand in a wave. She didn't look back, even though she wanted to.

O'Hara smiled at her uncertainly. "Are you and the sheriff…?"

"Friends?" Sadie asked lightly. "Sure we are. As I'm sure we will find out, you work a tough case together and you are either going to end up friends for life or sworn enemies. Let's go and get this helicopter, shall we?"

It was going to be a long trip. It was six hundred miles to the rig, and she wasn't looking forward to spending seven hours on a helicopter, some of it over an icy ocean.

As they made their way to the pad, Sadie tried not to think about Sheriff Cooper and the way he had just looked at her, much less figure out what it all meant. With the interrupted investigation this morning and his news that he was close to deciphering her father's map, she had enough going on. Right now, she needed to focus on getting out to the rig and getting stuck into this case.

She had a murder to solve.

And that meant there was a killer still out there.

CHAPTER FOUR

Sadie's heart was in her mouth as she stared out of the chopper window at the ocean below, feeling a mixture of awe and a primal fear of crashing into the icy, treacherous waters. It was a new feeling for her; as a native Alaskan she was used to the wilds, and as a special agent she was used to danger, but this far north the environment itself seemed hostile, as though they were trespassing.

This was no place for humans.

"Is it always this crazy?" Sadie asked the pilot without taking her eyes off the expanse of churning water below.

The pilot laughed, a dry sound low in his throat.

"This is nothing," he told her. "Especially for this time of year. Today, this is considered glassy."

Sadie said nothing, not daring to wonder what a less "calm" day would look like. She glanced over at O'Hara, who after seven hours of this looked as though he was going to throw up. Knowing the rookie agent would feel embarrassed if she were to point it out, Sadie wisely said nothing.

She hoped O'Hara wasn't going to be a liability. She barely knew the young agent and didn't have time to show him the ropes. The best way to learn was to do, in Sadie's opinion, and O'Hara's obvious nerves didn't bode well.

"There's the rig," the pilot said as a large structure appeared in the middle of the gray expanse of sea below. It was large, but Sadie thought it looked almost forlorn, and fragile somehow, as though the ocean could swamp it at any minute. Of course, that could just be the angle that she was looking from. Up here, the ocean overpowered everything.

"Finally," O'Hara murmured almost imperceptibly.

The chopper lowered quickly and circled once around the rig as it came down toward the helipad. Sadie saw the tower crane approaching—and the body, still swinging in the air. She was too far away to make out any details. The body looked more like a rag doll

15

than a human, tossed around on the winds as though it weighed nothing.

"Why haven't they cut it down?" O'Hara asked, sounding shocked.

"We need to get a good look at the scene of the crime," Sadie said. "Golightly sems to think there could be more going on here than meets the eye."

"It does seem like overkill for a dispute between derrick hands," O'Hara agreed.

That word again. *Overkill.* Sadie shuddered as she remembered Lawson that morning, and the way the woman's eyes had seemed to stare into her, laying bare everything that Sadie had hoped to be able to put behind her. The Mangler was dead, and she had hoped to never have to hear his name again.

The chopper landed and Sadie jumped out first, thanking the pilot. She looked around and saw a man rushing over to greet them. He must be the rig manager, she thought, or the "toolpusher," as the managers were known in derrick hand jargon.

"Agents, I'm glad you're here. The body is spooking the hell out of my men," the man said as he approached. He had the leathery, weather-beaten look of a long-time rig worker, with salt and pepper hair, keen blue eyes, and, underneath the heavy, layered uniform, what looked to be an impressive physique.

"I'm Special Agent Price, this is Agent O'Hara," Sadie said, flashing her badge. "Your name?"

"Jimmy Mason," the toolpusher told her. "I'll take you to look at the crane." He walked off, motioning for them to follow.

"He seems abrupt," O'Hara murmured as they followed.

"Not necessarily," Sadie said. "I don't suppose they have that much time for small talk up here."

As she approached the crane, a few of the crew were standing around, no doubt waiting for the instruction to get the body down. She felt their eyes on her as she approached and wondered exactly when the last time some of these guys had seen a woman was.

"How many crew are on board?" Sadie asked Mason.

"Twenty-two, including myself," he told her.

"And has anyone else been aboard the rig in the last twelve hours, or leading up to the body being discovered? Has anyone left?"

"No," Mason said, stopping in his tracks and staring up at the body swinging above their heads. He sounded a mixture of angry and bewildered, and Sadie wondered how it would feel to know that it had almost certainly been one of his crew who had done this.

Which meant that the murderer was still aboard the rig with them and hiding in plain sight.

Sadie looked up at the body, noting the bound hands and the grimace of horror frozen onto the dead man's face. With his skin blue with the cold, it was a macabre sight.

"Who is he?" Sadie asked softly.

The toolpusher looked sad for a moment. "Chuck Beeton. He is—was—our head engineer."

"Popular guy?" Sadie asked sympathetically.

Mason nodded, staring up at Chuck's body. "Yeah," he said heavily. She guessed that was as much emotion as Mason was going to show over the death of his engineer, but also that it was hitting him hard.

Of course, that didn't rule him out as a suspect.

As far as Sadie was concerned, everyone was a suspect until proven otherwise.

As Mason barked out his orders and three of the derrick hands began to carefully winch the crane down to lower the body, Sadie looked at O'Hara, who hadn't spoken. He was staring at the body as it lowered toward them, his face carefully composed.

"Is this your first time?" Sadie asked quietly, so that the crew didn't hear.

"No," O'Hara said, "but I'm still not used to it."

Sadie turned her eyes back to Chuck, now being laid carefully out on the upper deck. "You never get used to it," she told O'Hara. "You just learn how not to throw up. Trust me, you will see much worse than this."

Not that Chuck's body was entirely intact. There had clearly been a blow to the top of his head, what looked like blunt force. It was messy, but not so messy that she couldn't make out the distinct shape of the impression left. She stepped forward and crouched down, pulling on sterile gloves so she could carefully examine the wound, wishing they had access to a medical examiner. It would be some time before they would be able to get a coroner's report, so she was more or less on her own when it came to figuring out exactly how and when Chuck Beeton had been murdered.

"What is that?" O'Hara asked, crouching down next to her while keeping enough of a distance not to disturb the body. He peered at the wound with interest and Sadie smiled to herself. Perhaps O'Hara was going to be more of an asset than she had expected.

"It looks like some kind of a wrench," Sadie guessed. "But I'm not familiar with that exact star shape. It was a hard, clean blow, to leave an impression like that. Whoever wielded the weapon had some strength. We won't know for certain until the coroner's report, which could take a while, but I would suspect it was the blow that killed him, not the hanging."

Which meant that, just as Golightly had intimated, the point of the hanging was to give a very clear signal.

A warning. But of what?

She turned her attention to the rope, and to the complex knot.

"Mr. Mason, can I get your opinion on this?" Sadie said without looking up. Mason appeared, standing over her.

"What is it?" He was carefully avoiding looking at the body, Sadie noticed as the toolpusher crouched down on the other side of Chuck's corpse.

"I know this is difficult," Sadie said carefully, "but I need you to look at the wound on Chuck's head, and the knot on the rope. Can you identify the type of knot, and a weapon that could have made that mark? It's very distinctive."

And the weapon has to be somewhere on this rig, she thought to herself.

Mason's expression didn't change, but she saw the pulse in the side of his jaw and knew this was affecting him. He looked at the rope first, nodding his head at the knot.

"That's a French bowline," he said. "A type of nautical knot. It's used for hammocks usually."

"You would expect a simple noose knot," Sadie said thoughtfully.

"It's strong, a French bowline," Mason said, his voice gruff. There was a sheen of sweat on his forehead in spite of the cold. Being this close to Chuck, and the wound through which glimpses of Beeton's skull could be seen, wasn't a pleasant experience.

"So, whoever did this wanted to make sure as much as possible that Chuck wasn't brought down by the wind," Sadie said thoughtfully.

"He wanted the men to see him," Mason finished her thought, sounding angry.

"Is it a knot that is used often around here?" O'Hara asked.

Mason shook his head. "No." He sounded confused as he thought about that. "I only know it because I was in the Merchant Navy before I came onto the rigs. A few of the men might know it, but it isn't something we would ever have reason to use around here."

"Do you have any other former sailors in your crew?"

"Not right now."

There was a brief silence. Mason stared at the rope.

"I know this is hard," Sadie said carefully. "But I need you to look at Chuck's head wound for me. It looks as though he was hit by some kind of tool, but I don't recognize the shape. Do you?"

Mason inhaled sharply, looked quickly at Chuck's head and then turning away, staring into the distance with his jaw working furiously.

"Yes, I do." He took another deep breath. "It's a specialized spanner wrench. Only used for engineering. Chuck had one, obviously, and so would his assistant, Monty—Paul Montford, but no one calls him that."

"Thank you." Sadie got to her feet and both the manager and O'Hara jumped up eagerly after her, glad to be in less close proximity to what remained of Chuck Beeton. They were lucky, Sadie thought wryly, that the freezing temperatures meant that there was very little smell. The stench of dead flesh was something that, once it had gotten into your nostrils, would never quite leave you.

"I'll need to speak to Montford," she told Mason. "Can you think of any reason that he might have to kill Chuck?"

Mason looked angry again. "No one had a reason to kill Chuck. He was a decent guy. Quiet, hardworking. Best engineer I've had. Never had any trouble with him. But Monty…he's a hothead."

That was interesting. "In what sense?"

Mason looked around to check that the lingering derrick hands couldn't hear their conversation.

"There have been a few altercations with him over the past few years," he said. "He laid one of the derrick hands out a few months ago…beat the other guy bad enough to give him a concussion and put him in the infirmary."

Sadie raised an eyebrow. "He wasn't charged for that?"

Mason looked almost amused. "Out here, these things happen," he told her patiently, as though he was explaining to a small child. "The long hours, the loneliness, the lack of light…the lack of women," he added with a touch of embarrassment. "It gets to them. And to be fair to Monty, it was the other derrick hand who started it. Everyone kissed and made up in the end. But he does have a temper. I don't know if I would finger him for this though," he said, looking up at the crane.

19

Sadie wasn't sure either, but it was at least a place to start. And the fact that Montford had access to the suspected weapon currently put him firmly in the frame.

"I'll need to speak to him," she said. "Is there a space we can use? Where we won't be disturbed?"

Mason nodded. "The small galley. I'll go and get it prepped for you."

As he walked off, Sadie watched his retreating back, mulling over what he had just told her. O'Hara hovered nearby. Chuck lay at their feet, staring up at a dull gray sky that he couldn't see.

"Come on," Sadie said to the younger agent. "We've got a killer to catch."

CHAPTER FIVE

As Sadie and O'Hara set up shop in the small galley, waiting for Paul Montford to arrive, Sadie continued to question the rig manager about the engineering assistant.

"The guy that Montford put in the infirmary," she asked. "Was a weapon used?"

"No." Mason shook his head firmly. "Just fists. Monty is a fighter; he can look after himself. Most of the guys can, but Monty, well, you wouldn't want to cross him and then bump into him in a dark alley."

"So, you don't think he would be the type to use a weapon, if he and Chuck got into a fight?"

"No. But...if he was angry enough..." Mason's voice trailed off. He looked well out of his depth and Sadie felt sympathy for him. The harsh but steady rhythm of his days had been well and truly interrupted.

Mason left and Sadie and O'Hara sat behind the small desk that had been dragged in from somewhere. It had seen better days and the drawers were hanging off, but it would do.

"What do you think?" Sadie asked O'Hara, wanting to give the young agent a chance to use his analytical skills.

"Well, we haven't met Montford yet," O'Hara said. "But on paper he makes a good suspect. Access to the likely weapon and past history of attacking the other derrick hands."

"I can sense a 'but,'" Sadie said, nodding her head for O'Hara to continue.

"It's the whole business of the public hanging if he was already dead," O'Hara said. "It just doesn't seem to fit. What do you think?" He looked nervous, as though waiting for Sadie to contradict him. Instead, she smiled at him in an attempt to reassure him.

She was sure he went pink around the ears.

"You're right," she praised him. "Those were exactly my thoughts. If Chuck was killed as part of a brawl, or in an angry moment of revenge, you would expect the killer to want to cover it up—even push the body overboard if possible—rather than publicly string him up.

21

We're missing a lot here, but we've only just gotten started. Let's see what he says."

There was an awkward silence as they waited for the engineering assistant, and Sadie suppressed a sigh. She needed O'Hara to be alert and on form, which so far, he had been, but she also suspected that being starstruck around her might hold him back.

And she couldn't afford that. She needed to find out what had happened to Chuck so that she could get back to Anchorage and continue figuring out the mystery of her father's map.

And see Sheriff Cooper, a treacherous inner voice whispered.

Sadie ignored it.

"That was good thinking, questioning Mason further about the knot," Sadie said instead. "We've got twenty-two potential suspects here. If only a few of them know how to tie a French bowline, then that could be useful."

At the praise, O'Hara's ears went a distinct crimson color.

Just then, a man entered the room.

Paul Montford was not what she had expected from Mason's account of him. He was a small guy, average looking with keen, alert eyes. He nodded politely at them both before taking his seat and waiting for Sadie to speak. Unlike a lot of men she had encountered in her career, he didn't automatically assume that the man next to her was the one in charge.

"Mr. Montford," she began, noticing he was tapping his thigh with his wiry fingers. Nerves or guilt? "We need to ask you a few questions about Chuck."

"Ask away," Montford said. "Though I don't know how much I can tell you. I liked Chuck but we weren't especially close. I keep myself to myself. You have to out here, anything else would drive you mad. We're like a family, but a dysfunctional one, if you know what I mean?" He laughed, then stopped abruptly when Sadie didn't join in. His eyes narrowed suspiciously.

"What's going on here? Are you accusing me?"

"The rig manager tells us that you have a history of anger issues," Sadie said coolly. She could see what he meant. In just a few seconds Montford's countenance had changed. He sat stiffly in his chair now, his eyes glinting with barely concealed fury. She got the impression that he could attack at any moment.

"I don't suffer fools, if that's what you mean," he said. He exhaled slowly, clearly trying to rein in his temper. "But I wouldn't do something like this. A hanging? That's some intense shit."

"Chuck was killed with a spanner wrench," Sadie told him. "A type of wrench that your manager tells me that only you and Chuck use in your work here."

Montford had been looking at his hands, but his head snapped up at Sadie's words. "Mine went missing a couple of days ago," he said. He looked shocked, but he could be faking it. Usually good at reading people, Sadie wasn't too sure about this guy. It wasn't a stretch to imagine him snapping and killing someone in a temper.

But stringing the body up? That was the part that still made no sense in this scenario. There was something going on here, and she needed to find out what it was.

"When did you last see it? Was it not locked away?"

"Nah," Montford said with a quick shake of his head. "Why would it be? Like I said, no one but me and Chuck uses those wrenches. It was hanging up in the machine room. Yesterday I noticed it was missing. I've been asking the guys about it, because it's an important tool. I thought one of them had picked it up by mistake and assumed they would put it back when they realized." He paused, looking angry. "How was I supposed to know…?" He broke off, shaking his head again.

"Had you and Chuck had an argument recently?" Sadie asked. She was expecting Montford to be angry at the question, but he seemed to be expecting it.

"Nah," he said again. Sadie caught the edge of his accent but couldn't quite place it. "He's a pretty affable guy. Was," he added, swallowing hard.

Sadie eyed him. His grief seemed real, but could it be regret? If he had acted in temper…It was possible the whole hanging scenario was a way to deflect attention from a more mundane crime of passion.

"When was the last time you saw Chuck? I assume you both worked together as engineers?"

"Not always. Sometimes we're on separate shifts. We are this week, so the last time I spoke to him was about two days ago."

Sadie jotted that down on the notepad in front of her. She had a sharp memory and didn't need to take notes, but she knew from experience that the act of having their words recorded sometimes made people nervous. And nervous people were more likely to give themselves away.

"Can you remember what you spoke about?"

"Just work stuff. Nothing important." Montford sounded frustrated, shifting restlessly in his chair. "And speaking of work, can I get back to it now?"

Sadie eyed him coolly. "This is a murder investigation," she reminded him. "Unless you don't want us to discover who killed Chuck?"

Montford spoke through gritted teeth. "It. Wasn't. Me," he said loudly, enunciating every syllable. He leaned slightly forward in his chair in a way that could be seen as threatening and Sadie felt O'Hara tense in the seat beside her.

"That anger of yours is showing, Mr. Montford," Sadie said, raising an eyebrow. "Is there something you need to tell us?"

Montford stood up abruptly and began to pace around the room behind his chair, not looking at Sadie. She waited, motioning to O'Hara to do the same. Finally, Montford took a deep breath and sat back down. "I'm sorry," he said.

"What are you sorry for?"

"I know you need to ask these questions." He sounded deflated now. "But it had nothing to do with me and I don't know any reason why someone would want to kill Chuck. He was a decent guy, good at his job, and he didn't share much about himself. Most of us don't, really." He looked down at his hands again and Sadie wondered just how many secrets Montford was keeping about his own past. A guy didn't have this much coiled anger inside him without a few good reasons.

"Okay," Sadie said. "Just a few more questions. What exactly was the missing spanner wrench used for?"

"We use it on the shale shaker, in the machine shop."

"A shale shaker?"

"It's part of the solids control system," he told her. "We use it to remove cuttings from the mud."

"Mud?" Sadie asked, wondering where they were getting mud from on an oil rig. She had no idea what Chuck had just said.

"It's what we call the drilling fluid," he explained patiently.

"Right," she said, none the wiser but deciding it didn't matter. She wasn't here to learn how to drill for oil, she was here to catch a murderer. "Can you take us to the machine shop? I would like to have a look around." She stood up, slipping her notepad into the inside pocket of her parka. Montford nodded, although he looked none too pleased at her suggestion.

"Don't touch anything," he said.

"We might need to," O'Hara said, rising to join Sadie. "As Special Agent Price has pointed out, this is a murder investigation. We're not here on tour."

"Fine," Montford grumbled as he got to his feet. "But don't blame me if you injure yourselves."

He led them out of the room, across the upper deck and down wooden stairs to the machine shop. It was loud and noisy in there, although work stopped as they walked in, and the four men present looked at the federal agents with a mixture of interest and suspicion. Sadie knew she would need names for all of the crew, and as much background as was available on them. Right now, they had twenty-two subjects.

"This is the shale shaker," Montford said as he led them toward the engine. "The wrench would go here, see?" He sounded almost proud.

O'Hara at least looked interested, and Sadie let him get into a conversation with Montford about precisely what his and Chuck's jobs had entailed while she walked around the machine shop, her eyes peeled for anything that looked odd or out of place.

It didn't take long for her to find it. In the corner near a thin wooden bench pushed back against the wall she spotted a rag stained with dark fluid. It was a color and a shade that she recognized in an instant.

Blood.

As she leaned down to get a closer look, she noticed something metal poking out from underneath the rag.

A star-shaped spanner wrench.

She had found the murder weapon.

CHAPTER SIX

"O'Hara!" she called to the younger agent. Hearing the urgency in her voice he left Montford by the shale shaker and was by her side within seconds, watching in horror as Sadie pulled on forensic gloves and started to bag up the evidence. She had a basic forensics kit with her and could dust for fingerprints and scrape the blood, but it would have to go to the lab to be processed, which given their location could take days.

"Are you sure that's the right one?" O'Hara asked. He sounded shocked.

"Mr. Montford? Is this your spanner wrench?" Sadie asked, holding up the baggie. Montford had gone white.

"Yes," he said, "but it wasn't there yesterday. I told you, it went missing."

"Right, well, it seems to have reappeared," Sadie said grimly. She looked at the other derrick hands, who were all watching her with closed, wary expressions.

"Can someone fetch Mr. Mason, please?" she asked, and the nearest one to her nodded tersely and nipped quickly out of the machine shop. As he passed Montford he gave the assistant engineer a look of disgust. Montford blinked in surprise.

"This wasn't anything to do with me," he protested weakly, seemingly drained of his anger. His face had gone white with shock.

Mason appeared, looking grim as Sadie explained what she had found.

"I want Mr. Montford confined to his quarters for the time being while I investigate further," she told him. Mason nodded.

"Like hell!" Montford erupted, glaring at her. He stepped toward her, the rage coming into his eyes again, and Sadie very deliberately put a hand on her holster. Seeing the gun, Montford's eyes went wide.

"Look, I wouldn't hurt Chuck," he pleaded, looking from her to the rig manager. "I had no reason to."

26

Mason looked devastated and wouldn't meet Montford's eyes. Instead, he jerked his head toward the other derrick hands in the machine shop.

"Take Monty down to his bunk," he said. "We'll have to get a few men to watch him on shift."

Montford went with them without further objection, but the look on his face was that of a wounded animal about to strike, Sadie thought. She turned back to the rig manager.

"I need to have a look through Chuck's personal things," she told him. "Can you take us to his quarters?"

"Sure," Mason said quietly. "Follow me."

Sadie and O'Hara hung slightly behind the manager as they walked, talking in low voices.

"Do you think that's it?" O'Hara asked, sounding confused. "Just like that, we've got our guy. It seems too simple."

"Not for one minute," Sadie said, glancing at Mason walking ahead. "What murderer just leaves his weapon lying around like that? Wrapped in the victim's blood? It's a blatant set-up, and not a very clever one at that. But once Montford realizes that's what's happening he's going to be raging and I can see him tearing up the rig trying to find out who the culprit is. It's better to get him out of the way…and if the killer thinks we are arresting him, it will give him a false sense of security."

O'Hara looked impressed, and Sadie looked away, out over the ocean, feeling a sudden pang. O'Hara was doing fine so far, but she missed having Sheriff Cooper beside her. She could picture him in her mind's eye, trying to take charge, reining in Sadie's more outlandish theories and puffing his chest up like a protector whenever one of the derrick hands was the slightest bit rude to her. All the things, in fact, that usually drove her crazy every time she had worked a case with him.

She found herself wanting to talk to him about this and bounce ideas off him. The sheriff was a great cop, in her opinion wasted as a local trooper. But she knew he would hate being a federal agent. He liked being part of the scenery of Anchorage, protecting his part of the town and the hinterlands that stretched right up to the Chugach Mountains.

Mason led them down into the bunks on the eastern deck and into Chuck's quarters. As head engineer, Chuck had his own room—if you could call it that, Sadie thought. It was more like a large cupboard, with a small bunk, dirty sink, and a small chest of drawers with a clothes rail. There were no pictures or photographs, nothing to indicate who Chuck Beeton had been as a person. The room was so small they had to leave the door open just to get some air with her and O'Hara crammed inside, while Mason hovered in the doorway.

Sadie looked around at the tiny, sparse room. It wasn't much to leave behind, she thought sadly. It also wasn't helpful for her investigation, because Sadie liked to get a feel for who the victim had been. Who they had been in life, who they loved, who they hated, what they were scared of…the derrick hands were almost like ghosts.

She pulled out the chest of drawers, finding thermal underwear and shaving gear, and a large, ruled journal. She pulled it out and flipped it open only to feel disappointed when at first glance it seemed to be full of no more than professional notes and sketches pertaining to his position as engineer. Even so, she skimmed the last few pages.

Sadie frowned at the scribble of engineering notes, trying to make sense of them. One phrase kept appearing in a way that suggested it was important.

"Mr. Mason." She stood up and showed him the log, squeezing past O'Hara in the cramped space. "In the most recent entries, Chuck keeps talking about 'the jack-up legs.' Here it's even highlighted. With the date of two days away." She flipped through a few pages to show the confused-looking toolpusher. "Do you know what it means?"

"I might know what it means," Mason said slowly, "but Chuck must have known something I don't…which don't make no sense. The platform we are on is what we call a 'jack-up.' It's not fixed in place. The whole rig can be repositioned; that's what he might mean about the 'legs.' But if there were plans to reposition my rig, I would know about it." He shook his head. "I'll have to talk to corporate and see what's going on."

Sadie thought about that, tapping her fingers against the pages of Chuck's log, trying to get inside the mind of the head engineer. It was a difficult task when life on an oil rig was so alien to anyone outside of it.

But if Chuck indeed knew something about the rig that Mason didn't, that could be significant. Had Chuck been planning something? If so, with who? And what could be the use of a repositioning of the rig that wasn't authorized?

Sadie was beginning to realize that if she wanted to crack this case then she was going to have to brush up on her knowledge of the oil industry and how it all worked, because her gut told her, just as

28

Golightly had thought, that this was about way more than a simple feud between derrick hands.

She was about to question Mason further on the workings of the rig when they heard loud shouts coming from below.

"That's the crew quarters. Where Monty's been taken." Mason turned and jogged through the tiny corridors that separated the bunks and then led them down a ladder onto the lower quarters, right in the belly of the rig. Sadie followed him, her hand automatically on her holster and her body poised to fight. O'Hara was close behind her. She wondered what the rookie agent would be like in a physical altercation. He was fit, strong, but young and uncertain. His training at Quantico would have been exemplary, she knew, but it wasn't always about ability so much as attitude.

Not that she needed him behind her. Sadie had always prided herself on being able to physically take care of herself.

But even she took a step back when they reached Monty's bunk and saw the look on the man's face. He was grappling with the two derrick hands who had been assigned to watch him, and his eyes were blazing with fury, but it was a wild kind of anger that made him look almost possessed.

"Monty, calm down!" Mason yelled. Monty's arm swung out, knocking one of the men holding him onto the bunk behind them. He hit his head hard on the wall and cried out. Monty gave the other man a swift kick to his thigh and then whirled around to face Mason. He had spittle at the corners of his mouth and the tendons were corded and prominent in his neck. He looked like a feral animal, Sadie thought.

A cornered animal. There was fear behind that rage, she could tell, and she wondered briefly if Montford was claustrophobic, but just as quickly dismissed the idea. No one with that affliction would work on an oil rig where they had to live and sleep in such cramped quarters.

Then Montford spotted Sadie and his lips curled back from his teeth in what could only be described as a snarl.

"This is your fault," he hissed.

Then he knocked Mason into the wall in one swift moment and charged straight at Sadie.

CHAPTER SEVEN

Sadie braced herself, ready to tackle Montford. She didn't want to go for her gun, not in such cramped quarters with so many people around.

Suddenly O'Hara darted around the side of her, shielding her with an outstretched arm and aiming for Montford with the other. The rookie was quick, Sadie thought, although the attempt to play the hero saving the little lady routine irked her.

But if O'Hara was good, Montford was better, as the smaller man grabbed O'Hara's fist and twisted his arm, then sent the agent flying into the wall, knocking his forehead hard.

Sadie had had enough. As Montford spun around toward her, his pupils wildly dilated, Sadie tensed into a crouch and then, lightning quick, sent a swift kick to his thigh that caused his legs to go under him. She seized the opportunity to grab the man's shoulder and twist his arms behind his back as he fell, whipping out her cuffs with one hand.

She was expecting to end up wrestling on the floor with the enraged derrick hand, but as soon as he felt her knee in his back and the cuffs against his skin, the man went limp underneath her.

He had been in this position before. Sadie had seen enough to guess that Montford's reaction was something of a trauma response as opposed to a serious attempt to run away from a potential murder charge, so when she spoke to him her voice was softer than it might otherwise have been.

"Montford, I need you to calm down, okay?"

There was a muffled noise and a jerk of his head. Keeping firm pressure on his lower back with her knee, Sadie took a swift look around the cabin. Mason was helping the derrick hand who had been thrown onto the bunk out of the tiny living quarters, yelling at the derrick hands who had crowded outside to see what the commotion was about, to get out of his way. O'Hara was at her side standing over them, his gun drawn, with a nasty cut on his forehead. He looked embarrassed at having been gotten the better of by Montford rather than at all shocked or hurt.

The rookie would be alright, Sadie thought. He would shape up to be a damn good agent.

"I'm going to let you up," Sadie told the now subdued man underneath her, "but I need you to come with me back to the room we interviewed you in before, okay? We have a few more questions."

"I didn't do anything," Montford protested. He sounded as though he was about to cry, all of the fight having drained out of him.

"We can talk about that," Sadie said briskly. "I just need you to come with us, okay? Without trying anything. We're both armed and unless you are planning on jumping overboard and braving all that ice, there's nowhere you can go."

She took the jerk of Montford's head as a nod and hauled him to his feet. O'Hara glared at the man and Sadie suppressed a smile. The young agent's ego had been bruised.

She led him back up to the galley, Mason leading the way, while the derrick hands disappeared back to their various positions. Sadie guessed that not much work was being done on the rig today, but then, it was far from a normal day. It wasn't every day that a body was strung up on a crane.

Back in the "interview room," Montford sat hunched in his chair. This time, Mason stayed in the room while O'Hara went to see the on-board medic to get his forehead cleaned up.

"You want to tell me what that little psychotic break was all about?" Sadie asked.

Montford looked at the floor, then raised haunted eyes to look at her.

"The guys didn't want to sit and watch me, there's work to do, so they were talking about locking me in," he said, as though that explained everything.

Maybe it did.

"You're scared of being held captive," Sadie said softly. After her last two cases, she could relate to Montford, even if not in quite the same way.

He nodded, looking grateful that she understood.

"I was in jail before I came here. It was…as you imagine. I've never been good with feeling trapped. My dad…" He trailed off, not wanting to say more, but Sadie could hear the pain in his voice and

31

couldn't help her heart going out to him. There was too much cruelty in the world.

"What were you convicted of?"

"I got into a bar fight," he told her. "The other guy started it, but I lost my temper, and he got hurt a lot more than I intended. My wife left me while I was inside, my mom died, so I ended up here."

Sadie nodded. It was a typical enough story and fit what she had already gathered about him. Even so, she would make a point of checking his record. Sympathy or not, she wasn't completely ruling out Paul Montford as a suspect just yet.

"Okay. I just have a few questions. We went through Chuck's things, and in his notes, he keeps talking about repositioning 'the legs.' Mean anything to you?"

Montford frowned and looked at Mason. "The rig is going to be repositioned? No one told me that," he said, sounding confused. Mason shrugged in response.

"It was news to me, too," he said. Montford looked back at Sadie.

"I don't know anything about that," he said. "It doesn't sound right. If the rig was being repositioned, I would need to know. And Bossman here would be the first to know," he added, jerking his head toward Mason.

"Is it possible Chuck made a mistake? That he thought it was due to be repositioned when it wasn't?"

"Thinking about it," Mason said suddenly, "Chuck did say something last week about wanting to talk to me about the rig, but he's been on the night shift, so I've barely seen him since. But there's no way he would know about it first. It doesn't make a lot of sense, to be honest."

"Could Chuck's notes have been hypothetical?"

Montford shrugged. "Why would he write about it then? I wouldn't say Chuck was a 'hypothetical' guy."

Sadie sighed and ran a hand over her hair, smoothing escaped tendrils back into her bun. She was missing something, but what?

She was also starting to feel like she was at a dead end. There was no more to get out of Montford, at least at the moment.

"Who else would have been on the night shift with Chuck?" she asked the rig manager.

"Just a couple of guys in the machine shop. It's right at the other end of the platform from the crane, so…"

"So, Chuck could have been killed without them noticing," she finished for him. She looked back at Montford.

"Paul," she said quietly, and he looked up startled at the use of his first name. "If Mr. Mason assigns someone to watch over you and makes sure no one locks the door, can I trust you to behave?"

Montford nodded. He looked dejected now, as though all the fight had drained out of him.

"I liked Chuck," he said to no one in particular. "He didn't deserve this."

"I'm going to do everything I can to bring his killer to justice," Sadie told him. Then she stood up and addressed Mason again.

"Once Agent O'Hara joins me, I'm going to need to briefly interview each crew member," she told him. "I'll start with the two guys who were on shift with Chuck last night."

Mason nodded. Sadie uncuffed Montford and watched as he followed his manager back to his bunk. She felt restless, knowing she was on the wrong track but not yet having any other leads to follow.

There were twenty crew members to question, and the odds should have been good that something would turn up. That one of them, in fact, was their killer. Nothing else made any sense.

Yet a niggling inner voice told Sadie that the answers may not be on the rig at all.

*

O'Hara, a thick wedge of gauze taped to his forehead, groaned as the last derrick hand to be questioned left their makeshift interrogation room. "We didn't get anything," he said in frustration. "One of these guys must know something. I think those guys from the machine shop are covering up for each other. They were awake last night with Chuck, and the two of them could easily have subdued him and winched him up on that crane."

"Motive," Sadie said with a sigh, feeling drained herself. The questioning had proved less than fruitful and after a long day, she was beyond tired. It was still only early evening, yet this morning back in Anchorage at the investigation felt as though it had been days ago, not hours. "There's no motive. They looked genuinely blank when we showed them the knot, too. They all did. I don't really know what to think about what we are dealing with here."

"You still don't think it was Montford?"

33

Sadie shook her head. "We can't rule anyone out, but no. Like we said, the placement of the wrench makes no sense. He would have to want to be caught to do that, and I think we can tell by his behavior earlier that is the last thing he would want. And again, no motive. All we can really do now is to wait for the forensics and the background checks on the crew to come back. Time to make our way to whatever flea-bitten motel Golightly has secured for us. An early night is in order."

O'Hara looked nauseous at the thought of getting back on the helicopter.

Then Sadie's phone rang. Quite amazed that she could even get a signal this far north, Sadie answered it. It was Golightly.

"Found our killer, Price?" As usual, the ASAC didn't bother with pleasantries.

"No, sir," Sadie said. She was about to fill him in on the afternoon's events when Golightly said abruptly, "I didn't think so. I need you to fly over to another rig. It's about thirty miles away on the Beaufort, up towards Deadhorse."

Sadie sat up straight in her chair, suddenly alert.

"There's a suspect onboard?"

"Not a suspect," Golightly said, his voice grim. Sadie felt herself go cold as she realized what Golightly was about to say.

There had been another murder.

CHAPTER EIGHT

Sadie ignored O'Hara's retching in the seat next to her while the helicopter circled around as they approached the second rig platform. As evening pulled into night, the winds had raised, buffeting the copter as it descended. That, coupled with the sight of the violent churning of the waves underneath them, had been enough to make O'Hara lose his lunch.

"Sorry about that," O'Hara mumbled. He sounded mortified, and Sadie, remembering what it was like to be new to the job, felt a pang of sympathy for him.

"Don't worry about it," she reassured him. "You kept your stomach at the crime scene; that's usually where the newbies lose it. I puked up all over the scene of my first murder, the forensics team were furious."

O'Hara didn't look any happier with himself. "Instead, I just puke on a copter flight," he said with a sigh.

"We all have our faults," Sadie quipped lightly. O'Hara gave her a weak smile and then grimaced when the helicopter lurched again as it spiraled downward.

The flashlights on the platform just showed the silhouette of the body hanging from the hook of the flare boom as they approached.

"Seems to be the same," Sadie murmured, more to herself than anything. "What are the odds of two bodies found like this in one day? We've got a double murder."

"At least it safely rules Montford out. I don't know why, but I kind of felt sorry for him."

"Let's not rule anyone out for certain," Sadie cautioned, "but yeah, I think we can take him off our list of suspects for now."

O'Hara looked relieved as the helicopter landed and once again, they stepped out onto the rig to be greeted by the rig manager. This was one was a large, jowly guy with a distrusting expression on his face. Sadie doubted that he would be as helpful as Mason.

"Philip Cortez, I'm the manager here," he said. "I found the body earlier and called it in right away. Why has it taken you so long to get here?"

Sadie frowned. She didn't know herself. "It's only just been called in to us," she explained. "I'm Special Agent Price, Anchorage FBI, and this is Agent O'Hara. Who is the deceased?"

Cortez shrugged, looking distinctly uninterested. "Hard to tell from here. But it looks like the architect, he was visiting. All of my men are accounted for."

Sadie raised her eyebrows as she absorbed his words. "You're sure about that? Have you done a full head count?"

"Yes," Cortez said, sounding annoyed, "I have. There are thirty-four guys in my crew, and I've literally just done another head count. None of us have anything to do with this," he said defensively. Too defensively for Sadie's liking.

"It has to be the architect," Cortez went on. "He visited yesterday. There has been talk of expanding the rig. But I thought he had left." Cortez looked annoyed, as though pissed off at the inconvenience that the architect had caused him by getting murdered.

"Okay," Sadie said, deciding to get a look at the body before she attempted to question Cortez further. "Can we get him down?"

Cortez gave the order, and the crane was winched down. Sadie shone her flashlight on the victim. Unlike the first body this one showed no sign of being wounded in any other way and for a moment that gave Sadie pause. After all, coincidences did happen.

Then she spotted the complex knot that had been used, and knew they were looking at the work of one killer.

"Same knot," O'Hara murmured next to her. Sadie was pleased that he had been thinking along the same lines as she had. So far, she would be giving a good report on the young agent back to Golightly.

"The murders occurred within hours of each other, they must have," Sadie murmured to him. O'Hara nodded, his head tipped to one side as he thought hard. Sadie turned her attention back to the rig manager, and in the artificial light she saw how exhausted he looked. Perhaps he wasn't so much belligerent as tired, she thought. Managing a rig was hard work and they ran on a tight schedule; no wonder this murder was ruining his day.

"Just a few questions before I speak to your crew," Sadie said. "Have any unusual boats or helicopters been seen in the area last night or this morning? Could anyone unauthorized get on board?"

"No," the rig manager told her, staring down at the body. "Only this guy, who we were expecting. I mean, this is the Beaufort Sea, not the Caribbean. It's hardly a tourist hotspot. You have to know what you're doing to travel out here; these are some harsh conditions. We have a pretty high turnover of new derrick hands; not everyone can cope with it out here."

"I don't doubt that," Sadie said, glancing out over the bleak waves. "But if no one has been aboard, Mr. Cortez, then that can only mean that the murderer is one of your crew."

Cortez went white, and Sadie realized that the idea had only just occurred to him.

"That can't be right. They're decent, hardworking guys and I run a tight ship. Besides, who would want to do this? It makes no sense."

"The platform architect didn't get into any feuds or anything with any of the guys?"

Cortez shook his head again. "No, there was nothing like that. He made a few measurements, wanted to have a look at our output logs, and that was it. It was a routine visit before any expansion plans are finalized. I didn't think much of it, to be honest with you. We were busy as hell, so I left him to his business."

"You couldn't have known," Sadie said. "But someone has done this, and we need to find out who. Is there no way someone could have gotten aboard, or a boat of some kind could be missed?"

"It's possible," Cortez admitted. "Because we are so out of the way and the ocean is freezing, our security measures aren't exactly as tight as they could be, if you know what I mean? It's just not something you expect. But there was this guy last year…"

Cortez stopped mid-sentence as the sound of another helicopter cut through the air above them. Sadie and O'Hara looked up simultaneously.

"These guys got here nearly as quickly as you did," Cortez said accusingly.

"And who are 'these guys'?" Sadie asked as the helicopter landed just a few feet away.

"Well, the rig's holding company is British," Cortez told her. "So of course they would have been told about this first."

"Then that's why we weren't told immediately," Sadie said, resisting the urge to snap. Cortez was complaining that they hadn't turned up immediately, when they would have been far from the first people to be informed. She watched as the helicopter door opened. She had never worked with the Brits before, or rather, worked for them. They would be in charge of this one.

37

"So, these are British cops?" O'Hara muttered next to her, sounding bemused.

"Not just any cops," Sadie told him as a man and woman emerged from the helicopter. "These guys will be from Scotland Yard."

O'Hara inhaled sharply, sounding impressed, as Sadie assessed the two Scotland Yard agents now crossing the deck toward her.

The man was the older of the two, tall and with fine, prematurely white hair brushed back from a weather-beaten face out of which stared two astute blue eyes. He wore a suit under his thick parka and an air of quiet confidence. Next to him, his partner was a much shorter woman—even shorter than Sadie, in fact—with an iron-gray bob and bangs, in black slacks and brown shoes She gave Sadie an appraising smile as they approached.

"You must be FBI?" the man said, stretching out a hand to Sadie. She took it, feeling the cool roughness of the man's palms. He had a guttural accent, rather than the cut-glass vowels she had naively expected, and she wondered what part of the United Kingdom he was from. "I'm Detective Inspector Sheehan, and this is my partner, Detective Inspector Harding."

"Special Agent Price and Agent O'Hara," Sadie said. The woman made no attempt to offer her own hand as Sheehan moved on to shaking O'Hara's, but just inclined her head toward Sadie.

"When did you arrive on board?" she asked in an upper-class voice that was more akin to what Sadie had been expecting.

"Literally twenty minutes ago," Sadie said. "We were on another rig thirty miles to the southwest, investigating an almost identical murder. The holding company for that rig was American though. This was only just called in to us. As Cortez here has explained, they would have contacted you guys first. You weren't told about the first murder?"

"I don't suspect anyone knew," Harding said with a small frown of her carefully plucked eyebrows. She was an older woman, maybe early fifties, with a slightly stern air that reminded Sadie uncomfortably of Lawson from the investigation that morning. "Do you think they are connected?"

"At first glance it certainly seems so," Sadie said. "We'll leave you two to do your examination of the body and then perhaps we can pool our knowledge afterwards?"

Harding and Sheehan glanced at each other and then Sheehan nodded. "That sounds sensible," he said, clearing his throat.

"Is there somewhere Agent O'Hara and I can go to discuss things in private?" Sadie asked Cortez. "Preferably with a phone signal." She needed to phone Golightly to ask if he had known about this.

Cortez nodded and showed them over to a small machine shop that wasn't currently in use. They sat by the windows, watching the two Scotland Yard detectives as they appraised the crime scene. Although they were partners, it was Harding who seemed to be in charge, Sadie thought as she watched them both.

"Is this going to cause problems?" O'Hara asked. "Both the FBI and Scotland Yard being on the case, I mean. I haven't come across this before."

"Pray you don't ever again," Sadie sighed. She knew from experience that international disputes over the jurisdiction of a case could often be messy, derailing the investigation and wasting time as agents bickered with each other for authority. It wasn't quite as highly charged as the rivalry between Feds and local cops, but the stakes were usually a lot higher.

Sadie had no interest in getting involved in international pissing contests. She just wanted to find the killer.

Because if there was a second body, then there might well end up being a third.

At least.

"I'm not sure how it's going to work, but we need to liaise with them," Sadie told him. "Because these murders cannot not be linked, and we will all need to work together if we're going to solve this thing. Let's just hope our killer doesn't decide to target a Russian rig next, or this is going to get really messy. Murders, I can manage, but geopolitics are not my bag."

"Target next?" O'Hara picked up on her casual words. "You think he's going to strike again?"

"We can't rule it out until we know why these first two rigs were targeted," Sadie said. "But my initial thoughts would be that is something to do with either a territorial dispute or an environmental issue. More likely the former."

"Environmental?" O'Hara looked shocked. "That couldn't be a motive for murder, surely?"

"You would be surprised," Sadie said, staring out the window without focusing as she thought back to a recent case. One that had seen her very nearly lose her heart as well as her head.

Never again, she told herself firmly, and then ignored the image of a smiling Sheriff Cooper that came to mind.

"Of course, it could be something much smaller," she mused. "If we can find a link between the victims…it could be a lot more personal. We can't rule that out. But I would say this is all pointing towards something a lot bigger." She wondered what the Scotland Yard detectives would make of it.

"What if they don't want us on this case?" O'Hara asked, sounding disappointed. He had gotten the bug already, Sadie thought. The urge for justice and the need, once having begun a case, to wrap it up and bring some closure on behalf of the victims. To bring accountability on the part of the perpetrator.

"I doubt they will have much choice," Sadie told him. "This may be their rig, but it's in our territory. I wonder what Golightly makes of it all."

Right on cue, Sadie's phone rang, and it was indeed their superior. Sadie answered the call, although the line was crackly and the ASAC sounded as though he was speaking from underwater.

"…. Scotland Yard there?" Sadie made out through the static on the line.

"Yes," Sadie replied, raising her voice so that he could hear her. "What's the protocol?"

"They're in charge of this one," he told her. "The platform is considered British sovereignty. You're a consultant, in light of the first murder. See what ties them together. But don't let them take over everything. And try and keep it contained. This whole darn thing is getting too complex, and it needs to be kept out of the press, at least until we know what's going on here."

"Agreed," Sadie said.

"…any waves," her superior's voice came over the line, his first words muffled.

"Can you repeat?" Sadie asked, although she had a feeling she knew exactly what ASAC Golightly was about to say.

"…British Consulate are involved," Golightly said, yelling in an attempt to make himself heard. "So don't cause any trouble, Price. Keep a cool head."

"Of course," Sadie said, trying not to take offense. She had a reputation for being a stellar agent, but she also knew that she could on occasion be a loose cannon. She could hardly blame her boss for being wary. Even so, it rankled, and she couldn't help but wonder if the investigation into her handling of the Mangler had given Golightly reason to doubt her, even if subconsciously.

"We don't need any international incidents, Price," Golightly warned her again. "Just…solve the case."

The line crackled and went dead.

"What's happening?" O'Hara asked, looking worried. Sadie smiled at him, although her eyes were serious. She filled him in on Golightly's comments about the British Consulate and Sadie's role as a consultant.

"So, what are you going to do?"

"You mean," Sadie corrected the young agent, "what are *we* going to do. We are going to do exactly what Golightly expects us to do."

O'Hara frowned. "Which is?"

"Solve this case," Sadie said.

CHAPTER NINE

Sadie walked back out onto the deck, listening to Harding's questioning of the rig manager in a scene that could have been replaying her conversation with Mason that afternoon.

Harding was asking about the knot.

"...looks a little complicated for a hanging. Is it something used on the rig?"

Cortez looked puzzled. "No. I'm not even sure what type of knot that is."

"It's a French bowline," Sadie offered helpfully. "Used in nautical knots. It's usually used for hammocks."

Harding looked at her coolly, and Sadie got the distinct impression that the other woman didn't appreciate the intrusion. "And you know that how?" she asked in a slightly condescending tone that made Sadie's cheeks flush with annoyance. Four detectives on one case was going to be too much, she thought.

"It's the same knot from the earlier victim," she said quietly. Harding looked momentarily taken aback, before turning to the rig manager and firing questions at him. Cortez looked bemused, and Sadie guessed that the fact of an earlier murder was news to him.

"Any former sailors on board this operation?"

"No, ma'am," Cortez said, showing Harding a deference that he hadn't shown to Sadie. "Not that I know of."

"No one who would know about this knot?"

"You can ask, but it isn't one I've ever seen before."

Harding sighed, no doubt at the thought of asking the whole crew. "Agent Price," she said, "what similarities do you see between this body and the first? That's why you're here, isn't it?"

Sadie met her eyes, seeing a steel in the other woman that belied her prim and proper image. She wondered if Harding was the type of woman who didn't like other women, or if she didn't like Feds, or if this was just her personality. Sheehan was looking around, taking in the rig, seemingly oblivious to any tension. No doubt he was used to the superintendent's demeanor.

"The first victim was killed by a blow to the head before being hung," Sadie said. "But other than that, everything is identical. The knot, the crane, the fact it was all done so stealthily, everything."

"Any suspects in the first case?"

"Nothing solid," Sadie said, thinking of Paul Montford. "And I doubt any of the derrick hands from the American rig could manage two murders and then get back to his quarters without being noticed in one night."

Harding looked out across the ocean. "Then it must have been a round trip," she said.

"Meaning that they weren't inside jobs," Sadie said, finishing the thought for her. "Not unless there were two different killers working together...but how could they coordinate? And would two different people use the same obscure knot?"

"So, if we're looking at an exterior threat, that changes things," Harding murmured, more to herself than anyone else.

"It makes things more complex, that's for sure," Sadie said with a sigh. "Has anyone unauthorized ever gotten aboard?" she said to Cortez. Harding looked annoyed that Sadie had taken over the questioning of the man and Sadie bristled. She was used to being in charge of her own cases, not deferring to Scotland Yard or anyone else other than her immediate ASAC. Harding's attitude was starting to get to her.

Cortez looked thoughtful. "There's that eco activist guy. You know the type, always crying about fossil fuels. But this one's real militant."

Sadie shook her head. It would have been helpful if Cortez had thought to mention that right away.

"Is it possible that he could have sailed all the way out here?" she asked. *And between one rig and the other in less than twelve hours?* she thought, not wanting to disclose fully the details of the first murder. Cortez could be a suspect, however slim the chances.

"Oh yeah, the guy doesn't think twice about braving the elements." Cortez nodded, looking out over the now black ocean, huge swathes of floating ice glinting in the moonlight. "He got all the way out here once in an inflatable dinghy. Had to hand it to the guy; it's a pretty impossible feat. He damaged four pumps and the shale shaker before he was subdued; it took days before we were fully operational again."

"I see," Harding said coolly, cutting in just as Sadie was about to speak again. "And do we have any idea where he might be now?"

"Yeah. Last I heard, he was staying down in Deadhorse, making life miserable for everyone who doesn't live on darn solar panels."

Sadie exchanged a look with Harding.

"Deadhorse it is," Harding said primly.

*

O'Hara was doing his best to hold his stomach this time, Sadie noticed as the chopper took off once again above the Beaufort, heading for land this time. He was staring out the window, his jaw set and a thin sheen of sweat on his forehead. Sadie hoped the young agent managed to hold it together and not embarrass himself in front of Scotland Yard.

Sheehan put the phone down to his superior back in England and cleared his throat, looking slightly nauseous himself as the helicopter lurched through the night.

"The activist is called Ed Summers," he told them, "and he's known to us and to Quantico, thanks to his activities on the rigs. He has been arrested six times—jailed twice—for trespassing and sabotage. And he has managed to get on board and do damage on six rigs in the area." Sheehan shook his head with disgust, making his jowls wobble. "He should be deported from the area. He's on an international watchlist for ecoterrorism."

"Violence?" Sadie asked, leaning forward as she listened intently, trying to build a picture of Ed Summers. Environmental activists weren't her area of expertise.

But murderers were.

Sheehan shook his head. "No. Only damage of equipment. He's very good at getting on and offboard unnoticed though."

Harding sipped her tea thoughtfully. She was drinking it from the cup of a thermos flask, and Sadie suppressed a smile as she thought how quintessentially British that seemed.

"That doesn't sound right," the gray-haired woman said. "From damage to machinery to cold-blooded murder? And so publicly displayed? I don't believe we're looking at the same person."

"Not necessarily," Sadie cut in. "His behavior could be escalating if he isn't getting the reaction that he wants from the trespass and damage. Murder is usually built up to."

Harding raised a carefully plucked eyebrow at her, looking unimpressed. "Know a lot about this sort of thing, do you?"

"Yes," Sadie said shortly. "I'm an expert from the Behavioral Analysis Unit."

"How wonderful," Harding said drily. There was an awkward silence in the helicopter until Sheehan cleared his throat again. Sadie wasn't sure if it was part of his Northern English accent or if the weather had given him a chill.

"Anyway," he continued, "Summers has managed to board four of the rigs around the Beaufort Sea. His nautical skills are clearly quite something."

"That could explain the knot," O'Hara said. He was still holding his stomach, but his pallor had returned to normal. Sadie nodded. Summers was looking more and more likely to be their culprit.

"Yes, I thought that," Sheehan said. "But he hasn't boarded the rig where the first body was found before. So far, he hasn't targeted it, though I'm sure it would have been on his list."

"It's less likely that it's him then," Harding said, glancing at Sadie, who recognized that the other woman wanted to resume having the upper hand in the conversation. "He would have to be familiar with the layout of the rig to get away with killing someone and stringing them up."

"Unless he got on and off without anyone noticing," Sadie countered. Harding looked unconvinced, but Sheehan and O'Hara both nodded.

"He could have been doing a recce of the rig," Sheehan agreed. "Seeing the lie of the land before he struck. It would make sense."

"But why these particular people?" Harding argued. "If he was making a point about fossil fuels, surely he would target the rig managers? I say this is more about geopolitics, and we should be looking to the Russians."

Sadie hoped not. That was the last thing she needed to be caught up in. She could be stuck up here for weeks.

Away from Sheriff Cooper…and the possibility of finding out what was on her father's map. She had only been here a day, and yet her life in Anchorage seemed very far away.

"If this was something bigger, why target engineers and architects?" Sadie argued back. "Everything is a possibility, of course, but right now Summers is looking likely. Even if he isn't the culprit, he might know something. Is he part of an eco group?" she asked Sheehan, who was looking at her with what she thought was admiration. She got the impression that Harding wasn't used to being argued with.

"He used to be part of a group called Fuel Freedom, up until a few years ago," Sheehan told them. "But they were mostly a peaceful group, made up of students and aging Boomer hippies. It seems Ed Summers left when he couldn't convince them to take more direct action. Then he went solo and moved up here. And has been carrying out his antics ever since. Even prison doesn't deter him. If anything, it seemed to make him more dedicated."

Sadie thought about that. She had dealt with career criminals before—gangsters, mainly—who simply used a prison stint as a way to make new contacts and learn new strategies. It wasn't too far a stretch to assume that the same thing could happen with an ecoterrorist.

"But what would be the end goal of these murders?" Sadie mused aloud. "He can't expect to be taken seriously by the fuel industry like this. And as shocking as murder is, it doesn't do much to halt oil production."

"My thoughts exactly," Harding said as she screwed the top back on to her thermos flask. They were over land now and approaching the helipad near Deadhorse. Sadie ignored her comment and looked out the window. Deadhorse was far from well-lit and at this time of night Sadie could see very little. All she knew of it was that it was a tiny, isolated town, existing primarily to serve the oil operations in nearby Prudhoe Bay. It had an official population of twenty-five, although non-permanent employees of the oil industry made up another two thousand at least.

As they exited the helicopter, the Deadhorse sheriff was waiting for them. He was in his sixties at least, Sadie noticed, with a large gray moustache and weather-beaten skin. He didn't look impressed at being dragged out in the dark.

Harding took the lead, shaking the man's hand and introducing them all.

"I'm Detective Superintendent Harding, and this is Detective Inspector Sheehan. And these are Agents Price and O'Hara from Anchorage FBI."

"Special Agent Price," Sadie corrected, stepping forward to shake the man's hand. The sheriff looked surprised.

"Two broads in charge, huh?" he said. "Very modern."

"I had no idea it was still the 1950s here in Alaska," Harding said sweetly. Surprised, Sadie barked out a cough that she swiftly turned into a laugh.

"Do we have an address for Ed Summers?" Sadie asked. The sheriff nodded.

"This way."

As he led them into the town, Harding updated him on the case. O'Hara fell into step beside her, while Sheehan walked behind, looking at something on his phone and cussing at the intermittent signal.

"What's going on with you and Harding?" O'Hara asked in a low voice. "She's frostier than the climate."

Sadie laughed. "She's used to being Queen Bee, I think," she murmured. "I like the way she put that chauvinist old sheriff down though. She could be an asset."

As they walked past a small, derelict saloon toward a small cabin with cracked windowpanes, Sadie looked around at Deadhorse. It was tiny, all of the older buildings ramshackle affairs, with a few newer, gray buildings for the temporary residents. A lonely-looking motel stood alone at the end of the main track. It seemed an odd place for someone like Summers—apart from the fact that it was conveniently near to the oil rigs. He must have dedicated his entire life to the cause, she thought, to move out here just so he could be near his targets.

He obviously had no concerns about the authorities knowing where he was, which didn't fit with him being their murderer, she admitted to herself. Not unless he was already hiding out somewhere. Or, more worryingly, he was planning on carrying out a major attack that he would never come back from. The fact that they were using the word "terrorist" wasn't lost on her. She tried not to think about the damage and loss of life that explosives could cause on an oil rig.

"This is Summers's place," the sheriff said, stopping outside of the cabin with the cracked windowpanes. A tattered green and red flag clung to the fence that went around the porch, the insignia of a well-known environmental group. Sadie doubted they would appreciate being linked to this.

Sheehan noticed the direction of her gaze. "Scotland Yard want this wrapped up as soon as possible," he said. "Even though Summers is a lone wolf, the press will try and tie it to more recent climate campaigns, and this will end up being international news."

Sadie shook her head as the import of that sunk in. There was a global climate summit of world leaders approaching, and if this made

47

the international press it could be huge. The fossil fuel industry would use it to their advantage, and the protestors would no doubt react angrily. Whatever Summers—assuming he was the culprit—was up to, it could have far-reaching impacts.

Which, of course, was what he must want.

"Perhaps that's the motive," Sadie said. "With the climate summit approaching…"

"Like I said, geopolitics," Harding said. Sadie looked at her, then acquiesced with a nod. "Maybe," she conceded. "Maybe we're both right."

Harding looked surprised at that and gave Sadie a quick smile. She was actually quite pretty without her stern frown, Sadie thought.

The sheriff banged on the door loudly, and the sound reverberated around the track.

"Open up, Summers!" he yelled. "Got some folks here who need to speak to you."

There was no answer from inside, but Sadie saw a shadow flickering in the window.

"Someone's inside," she said. Harding nodded and stepped in front of the sheriff, rapping on the door.

"Mr. Summers," she said, her firm voice somehow carrying through the air better than the sheriff's yell, "I need you to open the door. This is Superintendent Detective Harding from Scotland Yard, and I'm here with the FBI. We need to talk to you in connection with two murders." She paused, and then said primly, "And if you don't answer the door, my federal colleagues here are going to shoot it off."

Ed Summers answered the door.

CHAPTER TEN

Sadie's instinct was to be the first to step inside the cabin and start interrogating Summers, and it felt counterintuitive to have to hold back while Harding explained why they were there. She took the time to have a good look at the activist, assessing his body language and demeanor.

He certainly looked the part, with long hair that was matted in places, as though he had attempted dreadlocks and then realized he didn't have the right hair for them, a straggly beard, and intense eyes that spoke to Sadie of an innate fanaticism that she had witnessed too many times in her career for comfort.

Fanatics were dangerous, regardless of their cause and even the righteousness of it. People who had something to die for, as Sadie was all too aware, were too often willing to kill for it too.

Even so, Summers looking genuinely bewildered by the appearance of the sheriff, Scotland Yard detectives, and FBI agents on his doorstep. As he let them in, he was blinking as though they had aroused him from sleep and looked bemused as Harding started to question him.

"We need to know where you have been for the last eighteen hours, particularly where you were last night."

"I was asleep last night," Summers said as though it was a ridiculous question. "And I've just been here today, binge-watching *Grey's Anatomy*. I have a crush on Ellen Pompeo," he offered by way of explanation.

"And do you have anyone who can corroborate that?"

"No," Summers said slowly. Now, Sadie thought, he was starting to look scared. "I've been here on my own. I live alone."

"How convenient. Or inconvenient, depending on which way you look at it," Harding said coolly.

Summers looked affronted. "Look, I haven't done anything wrong," he protested. "You can't just all turn up here like this. This is harassment, because of my past." He folded his arms self-righteously, gaining some confidence now. Harding looked far from impressed.

"Well, you do have a very *interesting* record, Mr. Summers," she said, her voice dripping with sarcasm. "In fact, you have gained access to oil rigs before, haven't you? And caused a not inconsiderable amount of damage. In fact, Mr. Cortez, the rig manager at one of our rigs attests to the fact that you have trespassed and caused damage on his platform before."

"Cortez hates me," Summers said, narrowing his eyes. "He has threatened to kill me before. Maybe you should be questioning him."

"Interesting you should mention murder, because that's precisely what we're investigating," Harding said.

Sadie watched the blood drain from Ed Summers's face. If he was acting, she thought, then he was good at it.

Harding kept up the pace of her questioning. "Do you believe that Mr. Cortez has the potential to kill, Mr. Summers? Is that what you're telling us? Do you have any reason to back this up?" Harding fired her questions at him in a staccato tone, giving him little time to think about his answers. It was exactly what Sadie would have done if she had led the questioning. Harding was good, even if Sadie felt reluctant to admit it.

O'Hara and the sheriff were listening intently but Sheehan, Sadie noticed, was looking carefully around the cabin. Catching Sadie's eye, he raised his eyebrows and jerked his head toward the far corner of the living area. Sadie followed his gaze, noticing a small pile of ropes and tie-downs.

With knots.

She was closer to the pile than Sheehan and so, keeping one eye and her ears on the conversation between Harding and Summers, she moved toward the ropes. As far as she could tell, there was nothing there that looked remotely like a French bowline. Of course, that didn't mean that Summers wouldn't know how to tie one. He had to be a good sailor in order to get about on the Beaufort in nothing but a dinghy.

"All I know is, I didn't do anything. You're targeting the wrong person. I don't kill people," Summers insisted. "I'm a non-violent resister."

"Smashing up machinery and damaging people's livelihoods seems pretty violent to me," Sheehan said in his gruff voice, sounding annoyed by Summers's claim.

Either his tone or comment or both got Summers's back up; his eyes went wide, and he glared at Sheehan as his face flushed with anger.

"Do you have any idea of how much damage the oil industry is causing to our planet and its people?" he yelled suddenly; his voice even louder than it seemed in the tiny cabin.

"Quiet down, boy," the sheriff growled, putting his hand on his pistol. Summers noticed the movement and pointed at him dramatically.

"You see. This is police brutality!" His voice became more high-pitched, and Sadie saw Sheehan roll his eyes.

"No one's laid a hand on you, lad," the older Brit said with a sigh. "You're the one getting all worked-up now. We just need some answers, that's all."

"Well, I can't give you any answers," Summers protested, although he quieted down. "I've already told you I don't know anything."

"I haven't finished asking you, so we haven't actually ascertained that," Harding said drily. "You got very upset when Detective Sheehan here referred to your past activities."

Summers shook his head wildly, and Sadie wondered if he was a little unhinged. Fanatics often were, living in a world in which their version of the world was the only correct one, or at least, the only one that mattered.

"Because it's a deliberate attempt to smear me as some kind of criminal," Summers said, raising his chin defiantly, "when all I have ever done is exercised my right to civil resistance against the ongoing degradation of our ecosystems."

"Trespassing and criminal damage isn't civil resistance," Harding pointed out calmly. "You seem to have different interpretations from the general public about what that means."

Summers made a scoffing noise in the back of his throat. "The general public believes what the media and the government tell them to believe," he said, a sneering tone in his voice. "The truth is modern civilization is destroying our planet. People will die in their millions if we don't stop burning oil, but you're not concerned about that, are you? Instead, you're out here chasing me around, one single activist, over a couple of derrick hands, nothing but pawns in the bigger game, instead of catching the real criminals!" His voice was rising again, and Sadie saw both Sheehan and O'Hara subtly switch their position into a stance more readily equipped to defend themselves if Summers exploded.

Harding seemed unperturbed; in fact, her gray eyes glimmered with a kind of triumph.

51

"Pawns in the game, Mr. Summers?" she echoed. "It doesn't seem as though you value the lives of the deceased particularly highly."

"Why should I?" Summers snapped. "What are two lives compared to millions?"

There was a silence in the cabin as his words lingered in the air. Summers's eyes went wide with horror as he realized how seriously he had just incriminated himself.

"Not that I think what happened to them isn't horrible," he gabbled swiftly.

"Are you sure? Because your comment sounded a lot like a confession to me, Mr. Summers," Harding said. There was ice in her tone.

"You're trying to entrap me!" Summers protested. He looked as though he was about to hyperventilate. Sadie wondered just how authentic his dramatic reactions were. She looked back over to the pile of ropes, noticing a small pile of clothes just behind them, in the corner. There was nothing too suspicious about that, she thought. The whole cabin was untidy, indicating the activist was less than domesticated in his home life.

Then something about the clothes caught her eye, a slight sheen in the light of the lamp. She stepped toward them to get a closer look, nodding to herself as she confirmed what she had thought. Then she turned her attention back to the interrogation.

"I'm going to ask you this one more time, Mr. Summers," Harding was saying, tapping her foot on the cabin floor as she spoke. She reminded Sadie of a high school teacher. The sort that could terrify the pupils with just a look. "Where were you last night and this morning?"

"I've told you!" Summers yelled at her, the tendons in his neck standing out. "I was here! The whole time! Watching television!" His hands had balled into fists at his side.

"Lower your tone and unclench your fists, sir," O'Hara ordered. "Or I'll have to cuff you."

Summers visibly softened his body language, but blew out a frustrated breath, his cheeks red. Sadie stepped forward, her eyes fixed on the angry activist.

"I have reason to believe you're lying, Mr. Summers," she said in a quiet voice. His head whipped around to look at her as four pairs of eyes swiveled in her direction.

"What are you talking about? I've told you already!"

"I'm assuming those clothes in the corner over there are yours? The waterproofs?" Sadie asked in the same calm but insistent tone.

Summers went very still, then he nodded, the movement stiff and jerky.

"Yes, they are. It is my cabin. So what?"

Sadie raised an eyebrow. "Have you worn them recently?"

Summers looked from her to Harding to the door, as though planning an escape route. O'Hara and Sheehan moved to block his way, and Summers stepped back toward the open inner door inside the cabin, nearly bumping into the sheriff who in turn moved to stand beside that door, effectively trapping Summers from making a run for it.

"No. I don't know. A few days…a week ago, maybe?" A pulse near Summers's right eye flickered rapidly. He was lying, but then Sadie already knew that.

Harding was watching Sadie keenly. "What's this about, Agent?" she asked. Sadie answered her, but kept her eyes firmly on Summers's face, watching his reaction.

"I think there might be something wrong with Ed's memory," she said in a conversational tone, "because those garments are sopping wet. He's been out in them very recently, I would say. Perhaps last night, returning this morning?"

A slow smile curved across Harding's face. "Do you have an explanation for this, Mr. Summers?" she asked in a satisfied tone that implied it was already a done deal; Ed Summers was their murderer.

The sheriff stepped forward then, jabbing a fat finger into the activist's face. "You murdering bastard," he growled. "We don't want your type in Deadhorse!"

The activist reared back, and Sadie thought for a moment that he was going to physically attack the sheriff. Instead, Summers saw his opportunity and ran through the inner door that the sheriff had now left uncovered. Immediately she, Sheehan, and O'Hara started after him, only for Sheehan to trip in the doorway as the sheriff jostled him out of the way so he could go after the activist himself, sending both the detective and the sheriff tumbling to the ground. No doubt the man didn't appreciate both out-of-towners and British cops taking over on his turf, but he had become a liability, Sadie thought in frustration as she finally got through the doorway after O'Hara to see Ed Summers halfway out of a back window.

"Grab a leg, don't waste time firing warning shots," Sadie yelled to O'Hara as she flung herself at the activist's retreating form, grabbing him around the knee. He kicked back, coming into contact with her ribs, but she hung on and twisted his knee, hearing him yelp in pain. *That will slow him down*, she thought, trying to ignore the pain in her side.

O'Hara was next to her in seconds, and between them they hauled a spitting and swearing Summers back through the window and cuffed his hands behind his back, forcing him to lie flat facing the floor. Sheehan was getting to his feet and dusting himself down, glaring at the sheriff, who had hauled himself into a nearby chair. Harding, who had stayed back from the pursuit, walked calmly into the room and looked down at the handcuffed activist.

"Resisting arrest is not a good look, Mr. Summers," she said. She met Sadie's eyes over the activist's now subdued form and nodded at her. "Good work, Agents. Let's get him down to the local station, and perhaps he can start being a little more truthful with us."

Sadie and O'Hara dragged Ed Summers to his feet and out of the cabin. All the fight had drained out of him now, and he turned his head and gave Sadie a mournful look, his eyes pleading for sympathy.

She ignored him. All she wanted to do now was get him safely locked in the holding cell at the local station and get some sleep before returning to Anchorage with a solved case behind her.

Except that Sadie had a sinking feeling that it wasn't going to be that easy.

It never was.

CHAPTER ELEVEN

Sadie watched as O'Hara thrust Ed Summers into the small holding cell and the Deadhorse sheriff loudly locked the metal door behind him.

"You'll be sleeping here tonight, boy," he told the activist. The sheriff was puffing his chest out, and Sadie guessed he was trying to claw back some dignity after taking a tumble back at the cabin and so nearly allowing the suspect to escape.

The local station was tiny, literally no more than a reception and a holding cell with an outside toilet. There was no interrogation room. Back home, Sadie was always teasing Sheriff and Deputy Cooper about their small station house, but it was a palace compared to this place.

"This cell stinks of piss," the activist complained crudely. He wasn't wrong, Sadie thought, noticing Harding discreetly pressing the back of her neatly manicured hand to her nose.

"Well, I'm sorry it ain't the Ritz," the sheriff hmphed. He took his seat behind the desk. "Are we gonna question him now, or in the morning?" he said, addressing his question to Sheehan. He still seemed to have some difficulty with the idea that Harding was the one in charge.

"With respect, Sheriff," Harding said delicately, "this is an out-of-town investigation. International, in fact. We can take care of the questioning. But in answer to your question, I'm sure Mr. Summers can wait until morning. I assume you will be here all night?"

The sheriff nodded stiffly, looking disappointed. "That will be a great help, you watching him for us," Harding said sweetly. It seemed to placate him.

Sadie wasn't so sure that Ed Summers should be left in the hands of the lumbering sheriff, but they didn't really have much choice. She had to trust the man to do his job.

"I'll need a DNA sample from you, Mr. Summers," Sadie said to the activist through the bars. He was sitting on the low wooden bench in the cell, slumped over, but his eyes were burning as he glared at her. He certainly had enough anger in him to kill, if tonight was anything to go by.

55

"You're not getting anything from me," he spat. "I don't know what you will use my DNA for."

"Well," Sadie said sarcastically, "this is a murder investigation, Ed. So I'll be testing to see if it matches any DNA found on the victim's bodies or on the weapons. It's a pretty standard procedure."

"Don't you patronize me," Summers snarled. "You're all working for Big Oil. You should be ashamed of yourselves. You're poisoning the planet, and all for your own lust for greed and profit. Psychopathic, that's what it is. You'd rather watch the world die than give up on your own comforts." He ended on a sob that seemed genuine, his face twisting up in despair, and Sadie didn't know what to say to him. Next to her, Sheehan stepped closer to the bars.

"This isn't the way, lad," he said, not unkindly. "I dare say you eco warriors have a bit of a point, but you won't make it this way. Violence never solves anything. And those men, they were just trying to make a living. Hardly their fault, now."

Summers stared at Sheehan, looking confused. "But I didn't do it," he said finally. "I didn't kill anyone."

"Let's do this in the morning," Harding cut in, her voice brisk. Sadie hesitated. She desperately needed some sleep, but she also felt that this would be a good time, while Summers was still discomfited from the arrest, to interrogate him. Waiting until the morning would give him time to both calm down and get a grip, and concoct a better story. She had bagged and tagged the wet clothes, but she knew it could be weeks before they were able to get lab results back up here. To wrap this up quickly, they needed a confession.

Still, she said nothing until they were outside the station and walking toward the rundown looking motel, where the sheriff had already arranged rooms for them, guessing that Harding would not appreciate being disagreed with in front of both the sheriff and the suspect.

"Perhaps two of us should go back and interrogate him now?" she suggested. "He's more likely to break while he's shocked and angry, than if we give him time to think about it."

"I disagree," Harding said, as though that were the last word on the matter, and carried on walking ahead. Sadie swallowed her urge to retort something and carried on walking, ignoring O'Hara's amused glances at her.

"She might be right," O'Hara said quietly. "A night stuck in that smelly cell being wound up by the sheriff...he'll likely be even more desperate by morning."

Sadie glared at him. "Traitor," she mumbled, then smiled at her own foolishness.

"I just want to get home," she admitted, trying to ignore the immediate image of Logan Cooper that came to mind.

"Yeah, me too," O'Hara admitted.

They reached the motel, which looked so dilapidated that Sadie wondered if it was deserted, until Sheehan knocked on the office door, and a flicker of light came from inside.

"At least you got a room to yourself," O'Hara murmured to her quietly. "I have to share with Sheehan. Judging by that cough, I reckon he snores."

Sadie shook her head in amusement as she stamped her feet and rubbed her hands together. She thought she was used to the cold but up here, so close to the arctic, it seemed to gnaw at the bones no matter how many protective layers she had on. She wondered if she would ever feel warm again.

A small, weaselly-looking woman opened the door and greeted them without warmth, probably annoyed that she was having to do such a late check-in. She showed them to their rooms and disappeared back downstairs without a word. Harding and Sadie were on the top floor, and Sadie gave O'Hara a rueful grin as she left him on the landing below and trudged up the stairs behind Harding.

One room was slightly bigger than the other. "I'll take this one," Harding said before Sadie could express a preference. "I need room; I have bad knees."

"Is that why you hung back when we had to apprehend the suspect?" Sadie asked sweetly, then immediately felt bad about the low blow. Harding simply regarded her coolly.

"You seemed to have it in hand, Agent Price," she said. "I'll stick to the actual crime-solving." She gave her a tight smile and then shut her door, just inches from Sadie's face. Sadie stared at the wooden door in fury, then stomped into her own room, feeling annoyed and tired and even—though she didn't like admitting it to herself—lonely. As she got undressed, she glanced at the clock on the wall, disappointed that it was far too late to call Caz and her daughter, Jenny, to say goodnight.

Instead, once she was as comfortable as she could manage on the hard, single mattress with a couple of scratchy blankets over her, she

57

called Sheriff Cooper. The signal on her cell phone was low, but she got through after a short pause.

"Sadie," he said, sounding both wide awake and pleased to hear from her. "How are things going? I take it you're staying up there tonight?"

"Not much choice," she said with a sigh. "As usual, things are more complicated than they first appeared. There was a second body, on a second rig."

Cooper whistled under his breath. "Definitely related?"

"Seems so." Trusting Cooper's sharp judgment, Sadie gave him a brief rundown on the day's events. He whistled louder when she told him that Scotland Yard was involved.

"Things are never simple with you, are they? Every case that seems cut and dried becomes immediately more complex as soon as you show up."

He was teasing her, but for once Sadie didn't find it funny, if only because it was becoming all too true.

"It's not as if it's me doing this, Cooper," she protested. "Although I am starting to wonder if I'm jinxed somehow."

Cooper's voice softened, and Sadie felt an ache in her chest that was about far more than just the cold.

"Don't be silly," he said gently. "You get these cases because you're the best at what you do. Who better to take them?"

"That's not even true on this one," Sadie grumbled, and proceeded to tell him about Harding.

"I get it," Cooper said. "You don't like working with anyone else at the best of times, never mind someone who ranks higher than you. It's an ego blow. Just as I was resentful when you were first assigned to a local murder case with me, remember?"

Sadie smiled at the memory of the first time that she and Cooper had met, eyeing each other warily over a freshly killed corpse. Then she bristled at his words about her ego.

"This is nothing to do with an ego trip," she said, and Cooper chuckled, clearly not believing a word of it. "I just don't like her. She throws her weight around and tries to take over."

Cooper laughed again and Sadie got the uncomfortable impression that he had once thought the same about her.

"She just stood there while the rest of us had to apprehend a fleeing suspect," she said finally.

"Well, that definitely isn't like you," Cooper conceded. "You're always the first one in the thick of things."

Sadie felt gratified. "Well, she is older, I suppose," she said, feeling more charitable toward her rival now.

"I miss you," Cooper said suddenly, his words rushed. There was a pause as Sadie took in his words, then admonished herself as she realized that she was grinning ear to ear at them.

"I've only been gone since this morning," she teased.

"It feels like longer."

"Yeah," Sadie sighed, looking out of the tiny roof window in her room. The stars seemed so much closer this far North. "It really does. I can't wait for this case to be over so that I can get back home, to be honest with you."

"And that's the closest I'm ever going to get to you admitting you miss me too," Cooper said wryly. Sadie laughed but felt herself blush at the same time. She *did* miss him. Why was it so hard to tell him that?

There was a brief silence, full of all the things that were being left unsaid, then Cooper cleared his throat awkwardly, reminding her briefly of Sheehan.

"So, I've been working on that map," he said, repeating his words from that morning. Was that really less than twenty-four hours ago? "I think I know the location he was trying to point to. He's definitely outlined the Lynx Lake Loop and the pine forest near the mountains."

Sadie listened intently. In his final moments her father had done his best to leave her a message, which she could only assume had something to do with her sister's death. It was information that she had been trying to get out of him for years, but he had remained tight-lipped until his last hours. The problem was that her father's map, drawn with shaky, dying hands, was crude at best. In a landscape where things could look much the same for miles, deciphering the exact area that he had been trying to point them to had been far from easy.

"Yes, but where he had marked the X there's nothing but snow and ice. We can't dig up the whole hinterlands. Assuming that's what we need to do and he's not pointing us towards an actual location or person."

Jessica's death had been at the forefront of Sadie's mind on her return to Alaska. Although there were other reasons she had asked for the transfer back home—the Mangler being a major one—it was the possibility of finally solving the mystery of Jessica that had been the pull factor. It had weighed on her mind for years, haunting her dreams, and she had seen her sister's face in every young girl she had interviewed, rescued, or worst of all, whose autopsies she had been present at. Jessica had been her world. Her prettier, smarter, older sister. Sadie had rarely felt resentful of her. Jessica was their father's favorite, but she had used that on many occasions to protect Sadie from his fists. After her mother's death from cancer while they were both young, Jessica had been the closest thing that Sadie had to a loving parent.

Then suddenly, one winter morning when her breath had turned to ice in the air, Sadie had woken up to find Jessica gone.

The verdict had been inconclusive. Ice preserved bodies well. Gossip flew around the small community of hunters, trappers, and ice fishermen on the outskirts of Anchorage. Was it an accident? Teenagers messing around, a wild night that had ended in disaster? Or had the pressure of an alcoholic, abusive father and a wayward younger sister pushed her over the edge? The unofficial verdict seemed to be that Jessica Price had killed herself. But Sadie knew better.

Her sister had too much to live for.

And she would *never* have left Sadie alone at the hands of their father.

Sadie had always known that her sister had been murdered, but a lack of evidence and leads had caused the case to be closed. Now, she and Sheriff Cooper were reopening it.

At first, Sadie had been excited, determined to finally get justice for her sister. She still felt that way, having nursed that determination for nearly fifteen years, but she also felt apprehensive, wondering if she was about to let skeletons out of the closet that could never be put back in.

"Sadie?" Cooper's voice came over the line and wrenched Sadie out of her reverie and back into the present. Cooper was still talking, but she had completely missed whatever he had been saying to her.

"Sorry, Cooper," she said wearily, turning over in the hard, scratchy bed. "I'm just exhausted. Say that again?"

"It's fine," Cooper said, almost tenderly. "I was just saying, I think we were looking at the map from the wrong angle. It's just a sketch, so obviously there's no scale or directions but I think I might have figured it out. But I'll wait until you get back to show you. You have a case to solve first."

Sadie nodded and then remembered that Cooper couldn't actually see her. "Yeah, hopefully Summers will confess tomorrow and then we can fly back. I'm sick of this place already. It's like no-man's-land, especially out on those rigs. I don't know how the men can stand it."

"You get used to a place, I suppose," Cooper mused. "Southerners probably say that about Alaska as a whole."

"True enough." Sadie remembered the comments she had received from her colleagues back in DC when she had informed them that she was transferring to Alaska Field Office. She was a rising star, a BAU expert, the woman who had solved the case of the Gestalt Mangler, and Alaska was the place that careers went to die, not flourish.

So far, she had been proving them wrong.

"Okay," she yawned, fatigue overtaking her, "I need to get some sleep. Tomorrow if you get time, will you look in on Caz and Jenny for me?"

"Of course. Goodnight, Price."

The call clicked off, and Sadie replaced her phone and lay in the dark, staring out the murky window. She hoped this would be the only night she would have to spend up here. That Ed Summers would play ball.

Except she still couldn't shake the feeling that they hadn't done this right.

That there was still a killer at loose, lurking out there in the dark.

Planning his next kill.

And it would be up to Sadie to stop him.

CHAPTER TWELVE

The howling storm winds blew right through her, threatening to push her right back across the rig as Sadie battled to cross the platform while trying to stay sheltered. She was alone and it felt as though the wind could blow her overboard any second, throwing her into the churning, icy seas. Sadie was a strong swimmer, but she knew she would stand no chance in the Beaufort Sea with its freezing temperatures, and in the middle of a storm that sent salt spray all over the decks of the rig.

She shuddered at the thought of going overboard, imagining herself desperately trying to fight against the waves, wondering which would kill her first, drowning or freezing to death. Imagined her body being pulled down by the strong undercurrents. Would she ever even be found? Or would she just go down as missing, and Caz, Jenny, and Cooper would never know what had happened to her?

Or maybe her body would turn up, floating to the surface, bobbing alongside the sheets of ice, bloated and blue, the ice making it impossible to determine exactly what had happened to her.

Just like when Jessica had been found.

Sadie pulled her scarf tighter around her face and crunched down, fighting against the wind. With every step she took the wind seemed to push her farther back, an invisible force that was stronger than she could ever be. Nature at its wildest and cruelest. The ramshackle cabins of Deadhorse would struggle in this weather to remain intact. Anything that wasn't battened down was being thrown about by the fierce wind, which seemed to get stronger with each gust. Sadie was beginning to wonder if she was ever going to make it across to the other side of the rig.

She couldn't remember, exactly, why it was that she had to do so, only that it was important, and if she didn't hurry up it would be too late…

Too late to save her.

Sadie was virtually crawling across the decks when she spotted a shadowy figure in front of her, heading toward the staircases that led up and into the storm. It was deadly out there. Whoever it was would fall. Sadie shouted a warning, but the sound was taken by the wind, not reaching even her own ears. She tried again, then stopped as she realized that she didn't know who the figure was. Moments before, she had been alone. The rig was deserted.

Was it the killer?

Sadie followed the shadowy figure, her heart beating a tattoo in her chest. She fumbled for her holster only to remember that she didn't have her gun.

Where was her gun?

Why couldn't she remember how she had gotten here, or what she was supposed to be doing, only that it was urgent?

There was danger here, but she didn't know where from.

She had lost sight of the figure and for a moment she stopped, bracing herself against the winds that were rapidly approaching hurricane status and peering into the darkness. She had no choice but to creep up the staircases and emerge out onto the top deck, only to be thrown off her feet and flung into the side of the rig with a force that knocked the wind out of her body.

As she groaned in pain, trying to right herself, she noticed that she was up the bottom of the boom crane. She looked up and saw the dark figure above her, climbing the latticework girders to the top of the crane. Were they crazy? Again, Sadie shouted for them to stop, but again she couldn't make herself heard. The wind was so loud now that she could barely hear herself think.

She had no choice. She had to go after them.

She pulled herself up the girders, lying as flat as she could against the metal, knowing that the winds would only get worse the higher she claimed. The place was a death trap, and it didn't seem that anyone was coming to assist her. But she had to carry on, had to follow the figure.

Had to save her…

Dread filled her as she watched the stranger scaling the crane above her, moving with surprising ease in the dangerous conditions that had Sadie clinging on for her life. For a moment, she wondered what the hell she was doing. The figure could be the killer, could be armed. Enticing Sadie to the top of the crane so that she could be the next victim.

But it didn't matter. She was compelled to go on. She wondered who would find her body in the morning.

Using all of her strength she dragged herself up the crane, step by step, staying as flat as she could and bracing herself against the hurricane. She was moving at a snail's pace and had lost sight of the stranger now. Were they at the top of the crane?

Waiting for her?

She let out a scream as her foot suddenly slipped on the wet metal, only just stopping herself from plunging onto the deck below. She was higher than she realized, and she could feel the crane swaying, high above the ocean. Feeling dizziness wash over her, she closed her eyes and held on tight, willing herself not to fall.

Then a noise above made her look and she saw the figure, black against the charcoal sky but unmistakable, plunging toward her.

Jumping or falling?

Steadying herself as best she could, Sadie wrapped an arm and a leg around the girder and tried to reach it in a desperate attempt to grab on to the falling figure as they threatened to hurtle right past her.

Then suddenly they jerked upwards, out of sight, and then they were there again, somehow suspended in midair.

Floating in the air. Just inches away from her. But that was impossible.

Then above her, she saw the rope.

The figure was hanging from a rope. Tied with a knot that she recognized...

The wind seemed to disappear as suddenly as it had come. The figure—no, she realized with a stab of horror—the body, was turning at the end of the rope. Turning its face toward her. *No...*

Sadie grabbed hold of the girder, panting as a wave of nausea washed over her. She didn't want to see this, but no matter how hard she tried she found that she couldn't look away. Couldn't tear her eyes from the face that spun round toward her, its unseeing eyes bulging and tongue hanging out of its mouth that was stretched in a diabolical grin. It was a face that Sadie knew as well as she knew her own.

Jessica.

Once again, Sadie hadn't been able to save her.

Sadie screamed.

And screamed.

She was still screaming when she sat upright in bed, her heart pounding as she stared around the room, her eyes wild, her hands reaching out for her sister.

Gradually her surroundings came into focus. She wasn't on the rigs. She was in the Deadhorse motel, in a scratchy little bed in the attic. She was safe.

And her sister was still dead.

A sob ripped through her, and she buried her head in her hands. They were shaking.

Outside, the wind howled, rattling the small window in its frame. That part had been real, at least.

She wrapped the scratchy blanket around herself, shuddering against the early morning chill, hoping that Harding hadn't heard her screaming. She really needed to talk to someone about these nightmares. They were happening all the time now, especially when she had a new case. The present constantly mingling with the past and dreaming up ever more frightening scenarios.

She rubbed her calves where they were stiff from sleep, trying to ground herself and focus her mind on the day ahead. On anything but her dream.

Swinging her legs over the edge of the bed, Sadie washed as best as she could at the small basin which produced a trickle of tepid water, and then dressed rapidly, pulling on as many layers as she could. Up here, the cold was bone deep. She thought longingly of the fires that she and Caz sometimes built out behind the saloon, roasting marshmallows with little Jenny.

At the thought of food, her stomach rumbled. She had barely eaten the day before and felt that she could easily eat a horse.

When she reached the tiny area downstairs though she saw that Harding and Sheehan had beaten her to it and were hungrily devouring what looked like eggs and reindeer sausage.

"Please tell me there's some more," she said, her mouth salivating at the smell.

"Loads. I'm on my second helping," Sheehan told her through a mouthful of food. "You guys know how to cook a sausage; I'll give you that."

"It's reindeer," she told him, and she went to poke her head through the serving hatch to order her own breakfast. Sheehan looked startled, staring suspiciously at the meat on his fork.

Sadie joined them at the table with a plate of food to see Harding looking at her with an unreadable expression.

"How did you sleep, Agent Price?"

65

"Fine, thank you," Sadie snapped, then felt guilty as Harding's tone had held a hint of genuine concern. But she was in no mood to disclose her deepest secrets to the British detectives.

Luckily O'Hara chose that moment to make an appearance, looking rumpled and still half asleep as he fetched his own breakfast. He joined them at the table, yawning loudly.

"Any word from that sheriff? Has Summers confessed?" he asked hopefully. The young rookie was as eager to get home as Sadie was.

"No," Sheehan said through a mouthful of reindeer, "but we will get straight down there after we have finished eating. After a night in that smelly cell, I'm sure he'll will be grateful to see us." He chuckled to himself, finding the idea amusing. Sadie felt less hopeful, remembering her reservations the night before, but perhaps she was still unsettled by the vividness of her nightmare. She always felt anxious the morning after she had one, resisting the urge to jump at shadows. It was a problem, because murder investigations required her to be in top form.

"Right, let's go," Harding said as she placed her knife and fork down. Sadie shoveled the rest of her breakfast down, took a swig of black coffee, and got up, ready to go. They thanked the motel owner, who looked slightly less sour after they all complimented her on the food, and made their way to the station. Sadie was glad to see that the winds had calmed.

O'Hara banged on the door of the tiny station, but there was no answer. Frowning, he banged again.

"I heard something," Sadie said. "Like a groaning?"

Sheehan tried the door, and it opened to show a scene that none of them had been expecting to see that morning.

Sadie swept her eyes around the inside of the station, hardly able to comprehend what she was seeing. The reception desk was empty, and the sheriff was inside the cell, a gash on his forehead, bright red with rage and embarrassment as he saw them entering.

There was no sign of Ed Summers.

"What the hell?" O'Hara was first inside, rushing to the cell. It was locked.

"There's a spare key in my desk," the sheriff mumbled, avoiding everybody's eyes.

"And just what happened here?" Harding demanded, although Sadie felt sure that she could make a fair guess. She rummaged in the drawer under the reception desk, found the key on a chain, and tossed it to O'Hara, who unlocked the cell door and let the Deadhorse sheriff out. Harding had her hands on her hips, reminding Sadie yet again of a strict high school teacher, while O'Hara had a look of incredulous disgust on his face and Sheehan was coughing in a way that suggested that he was trying to cover up laughter.

"The bastard," the sheriff wheezed. "He got the better of me."

"And just how did he do that?" There was zero sympathy in Harding's tone.

"He said he was feeling ill," the sheriff said, talking too fast in a way that made Sadie wonder if he was entirely telling the truth. "He was doubling over groaning, sounding like he was in agony. Said he had a stomach ulcer and it had burst and I had to get him an air ambulance or he could be dead within minutes. Well, I couldn't just ignore that, could I? So I went in with the first aid kit, but the minute I stepped inside he pushed me into the bars from behind, tripped me up, and he had the key off me before I had any chance of reaching for a gun."

The four of them stared at him, taking in his somewhat fantastic story. Sheehan looked thoughtful.

"When I checked on Ed Summers's record, it mentioned he was a martial artist."

Harding glared at her partner.

"It would have been a good idea to mention that, perhaps?" Sheehan shrugged, looking chastened, while Harding's angry eyes swiveled back to the sheriff. "Then perhaps our brave sheriff here might have thought twice before he stepped inside the cell alone."

Sadie suppressed a smile. In spite of herself, there were moments when she couldn't help liking Harding.

"Do you need medical attention for that cut on your head?" Sadie asked the sheriff, unable to help feeling just a little sorry for him. The sheriff shook his head mournfully.

"No, it just dazed me momentarily, that's all."

"Right," Harding said briskly. "Do we have any idea where Summers may have gone?"

"To the coast, I'm guessing," Sadie said. "Trying to escape by land around here would take too long and be just as dangerous as the seas. If his record is anything to go by then he's an accomplished sailor. I reckon he would try to get to his dinghy. Could he have taken a cab? Are there any drivers who would take him anywhere this early in the morning?"

The sheriff looked even more embarrassed. "I heard him drive off in the police cruiser," he said. "All my keys were on the same chain."

Sadie exchanged a glance with Harding, who rolled her eyes in exasperation. The morning was going from bad to worse.

"How long ago did this happen?"

"At least an hour ago." The Deadhorse sheriff looked so miserable that Sadie would have felt some sympathy for him if he hadn't messed things up quite so badly.

"I'll get a helicopter arranged," she said, reaching for her phone. "We need to try and head him off."

Before we lose him, she thought. Her eyes met Harding, and they shared a look that indicated the older detective was thinking the exact same thing as she was.

That if Ed Summers managed to escape them, then he was free to kill again.

And with his apparent skills at getting on and off the oil rigs unnoticed, all of the local derrick hands were no more than sitting ducks.

"We have to stop him," Sadie said out loud. Harding gave a brisk nod.

"Let's go," she said.

CHAPTER THIRTEEN

This one was going to be risky.

It was early morning, but some of the derrick hands would already be up and about on this rig, and it was going to take all of his carefully honed skills to avoid them. He couldn't afford to get caught.

He had too much work to do if he was going to achieve his mission. Anger at the fossil fuel industry and all those who worked in it filled him with a white-hot conviction. His victims were nobodies, mere tools in his larger mission, but at the same time he knew that they deserved to die, and so he felt neither sympathy nor remorse. They had made their choice when they agreed to the job. Agreed to use their skills to help poison the Earth and the oceans without a care for the consequences.

His anger kept him going. He used its energy to propel him forward and keep him sharp.

Keep him focused.

These were dangerous missions, but he wasn't worried about himself. He was prepared to make sacrifices for the larger cause. But he needed to be able to keep going.

The dark was his friend as he claimed one of the stanchions on the main platform, using the mountain climbing gear that he had purchased for exactly this purpose. He tried not to think about just how high above the ocean he was. The Beaufort swirled underneath him, and he had a sudden image of it as a hungry predator, patiently biding its time for him to fall so it could claim him in its icy depths.

But that wasn't going to happen. Not today. He was good on the ocean, expertly maneuvering the small dinghy across its treacherous expanse, using the dark and the cold to his advantage. He thought of the Beaufort Sea as his friend, but at moments like this he was acutely aware that the ocean didn't care who it claimed; derrick hand or activist.

Finally, he reached the top of the stanchion and heaved himself on the platform, crouching down so as not to be seen.

Now for the hard part.

He left the climbing gear looped over the top of the stanchion, ready to make his escape, and started to make his way along the terrace, his eyes on the farthest top deck, where he knew his target would be. He had been here before, unseen, observing. No one ever expected him. Who would be crazy enough to try this?

But from now on he was going to have to be more careful, as word of the earlier murders was getting around quicker than he had anticipated.

Moving at a crouch, he made his way across the terracing on the lower deck, his eyes peeled for derrick hands. He could see a few in the distance, over at the machine shop, and he did his best to blend with the shadows. Dressed all in black, only his eyes visible over the black scarf wrapped around his head and face, it was easy enough to creep through the Alaskan dark unseen, as long as he kept out of the way of the headlamps worn by the derrick hands.

He could see the crane up ahead, and he already knew that it was largely out of sight of the machine shop. As long as he stuck to his planned route and timing, and nothing went awry, he could display this body as he had the last two. That touch was important, he thought. The drama of it. The style of execution.

Because that's what these killings were. He wasn't a murderer.

He was a dealer of justice.

He moved carefully, with practiced ease, keeping his breath even and silent. He reached his destination and slipped inside the interior, moving quickly down the corridor, knowing that he wouldn't have long now before he was seen.

He lifted his gun with its silencer from over his shoulder and held it in his hands, ready to use it if he was surprised. It didn't really matter, as long as he got back off the rig, unseen by anyone left alive.

Reaching the room that he was headed for, he let himself in, gun held out in front of him.

The man was already up and awake, sitting at a tiny desk with a dull lamp illuminating a newspaper that he was reading, wearing an expensive suit that must have cost more than a month's worth of derrick hand wages.

The man was a fitting target, a living symbol of everything that he opposed, and a smile curved the killer's lips as he thought that he would enjoy this one.

The man looked up, surprised but with an automatic polite smile on his jowly face. His eyes widened and then bulged as he saw the gun, and his mouth opened and closed like a fish, with only a frightened gargle coming out. Too scared to even beg for his life. The killer's smile widened. The impotent fear coming off the man in waves energized him. Out of all of them, this one deserved to die the most.

It was a shame that he didn't have time to be more creative; to make the man's fear last. To make him suffer the way his actions were making so many others suffer, with reverberations that were unthinkable.

This wasn't murder. This was justice.

With a feeling of supreme righteousness, he pulled the trigger.

CHAPTER FOURTEEN

In the helicopter once again, Sadie stared out the window at the meandering contours of the coastal road below, her eyes peeled for any sign of the police cruiser. They were heading for Prudhoe Bay, the nearest place that Ed Summers would be likely to set off from and where his dinghy was most likely kept.

Sadie had put her initial reservations about Summers to one side. Everything pointed to him being the killer. He had both the means and the motive, and previous convictions for trespassing and causing trouble on the rigs. Add to that the wet clothes and the breaking out of jail, and it seemed a sure bet. She wondered what had made him escalate from vandalism to murder so quickly.

Taking her eyes off the icy expanse below, Sadie looked around the interior of the chopper. Harding was once again drinking tea from her thermos, which was perfectly balanced on her lap in spite of the jerky motion of the helicopter. It was an impressive skill.

O'Hara had his eyes shut and he had gone gray. He really needed to get used to flying and get a stronger stomach. Sheehan was tapping his fingers on his thigh, deep in thought.

"I reckon he was lying," he said to no one in particular. Sadie frowned.

"Who? Summers?"

"No." Sheehan shook his head. "That sheriff. I don't think he would have cared about Summers claiming to be sick. I reckon he decided to have a go at interrogating him by himself."

Harding looked up, sipping her tea delicately.

"You may very well be right," she said to her colleague. "That man is an obvious loose cannon. I should have left one of us with him overnight to supervise the prisoner." She looked annoyed at herself for not anticipating the Deadhorse sheriff's stupidity.

Sadie didn't reply, suspecting that Harding would have volunteered Sadie or O'Hara before her own detective. She bit back the urge to remind the older woman that she wasn't her direct superior, remembering Golightly's warning not to antagonize the Brits. Perhaps

Cooper was right, and she really did have a bigger ego than she had thought.

"He weren't the sharpest tool in the box," Sheehan went on, "but we shouldn't have had to supervise him in his own jurisdiction. Not your fault," he said to Harding.

"I agree," Sadie said with a sigh. "I didn't think the sheriff was being entirely truthful. He was obviously embarrassed. But it's too late to do anything now. We need to focus on catching Summers."

O'Hara opened his eyes and made a grunting sound of agreement, then hurriedly closed them again. Sadie suppressed a smile. The rookie was really suffering with all this time in the air.

"We can only hope that we are able to catch him before he heads back out to sea," Harding said, setting her thermos down and looking out the window herself as the chopper tipped slightly to one side. They weren't far from Prudhoe Bay and the chances of intercepting Summers were looking more and more remote.

Sheehan nodded. "If he's taken his dinghy, it's going to be impossible to find him over the open water."

"If he's in the dinghy, he might strike another one of the rigs," Sadie cut in. Harding looked at her with an expression that indicated she didn't think much of Sadie's suggestion.

"I appreciate that he's likely to kill again very soon, but right now, knowing that we are onto him and looking for him? He's a fugitive."

"Exactly," Sadie argued. "He doesn't have much else left to lose."

Harding raised an eyebrow at her in a way that Sadie had come to recognize meant the woman was going to say something that would infuriate her. "This what they teach you in your Behavioral Analysis classes, is it?"

O'Hara opened his eyes, his airsickness momentarily forgotten as he looked at Sadie, waiting for her to respond to Harding's dig.

Sadie smiled patiently, although she felt hot with anger at the woman's condescending tone. "Summers has nowhere to realistically go other than the rigs," she pointed out. "I don't care how good a sailor he is; he isn't going to last too long out on that dinghy in the middle of winter, not on the Beaufort. We can't man the entire coast, but there aren't many places where it would be safe for him to come ashore, not that are within a few days' sailing distance. Summers believes in his cause. It's bigger than him. Whatever he believes his overall mission is, he will want to accomplish it before he is apprehended."

Sheehan nodded in agreement. "I reckon the lass is right," he said, his accent thick and completely different from Harding's clipped tones. It was almost funny how she had always naively expected all British people to sound the same, Sadie thought.

Harding glared at her partner before giving a dignified shrug.

"You know this coastline better than we do," she acquiesced. "So you may well be right, in that case. We're nearly at the shore. Perhaps you could call ahead and get the Prudhoe sheriff to meet us?"

Figuring that was the closest that she was going to get to an apology from Harding, Sadie made the call. Prudhoe Bay had already been alerted as to Summers's escape and Sadie held out hope that the local sheriff was going to tell her that the police cruiser Summers had stolen had been located, but that was quickly dashed. There was no sign of either Summers or the missing vehicle.

The helicopter landed close to Prudhoe Bay's small fishing wharf. "The fishermen might know Summers," Sadie said. "We should question them."

"Yes, I agree. Sheehan and Agent O'Hara can do that. You and I, Agent Price, will talk to the sheriff. Hopefully he will have more wits about him than the fool at Deadhorse."

Sadie would rather have stayed with O'Hara, or at least been asked rather than ordered, and was about to retort when she caught O'Hara's eye and thought better of it. The young agent wanted to get home, and so did she. The sooner this was over, the sooner she would never have to see Superintendent Harding again.

Cooper and Golightly would be proud of her, she thought with a wry smile to herself. She wasn't exactly known for keeping her temper.

O'Hara and Sheehan headed off toward the wharf while she followed Harding to where the Prudhoe Bay sheriff was standing with the Coast Guard. He nodded in greeting, extending a hand to Sadie first. Harding didn't look pleased.

"Special Agent Price, Anchorage FBI," Sadie introduced herself. "This is—"

"Detective Superintendent Harding," the older woman cut in before Sadie could finish. "I'm with Scotland Yard. The last body was found on one of our rigs, so this is now a British matter."

The sheriff looked less than impressed. He was a younger, fitter man than the Deadhorse sheriff, with intelligent gray eyes over a hooked nose and sparse moustache. He had the lean, hard look that Sadie often saw in Alaskan men who were used to the harsh climate;

thrived on it, even. He wouldn't generally welcome the intrusion of either Scotland Yard or the FBI, Sadie guessed, thinking again of Cooper back home at Anchorage.

"Seems to me it's a matter for all of us," the Prudhoe sheriff said coolly. "No one wants a murderer running around, especially if he's targeting derrick hands. There's a lot of them around here. Not that they're popular with the fishermen. Oil spills," he added by way of explanation.

Sadie nodded with understanding. Local oil spills could badly affect the chances of fishermen making a living, especially the independent fishermen with smaller trawlers. Exposure to oil made fish unsafe for human consumption and could also have long-term effects on the fish population, by impairing reproduction and eroding fins, enlarging fish livers, and causing a reduction in growth. In an area where living was for so many often about survival, oil spills could be as deadly to the fishermen and their families as they were to the fish.

"We need to find Ed Summers," Harding said impatiently, uninterested in oil spills on the Alaskan coast. "We have reason to believe he's headed straight for his next victim." As though that had been her reasoning and not Sadie's. Sadie jammed her hands in her pockets and looked at the snow below her feet. Had she ever come across so goddamn infuriating to the Coopers?

"I can get the nearest cutter on standby," the Coast Guardsman said, speaking for the first time. Harding was about to respond when they saw O'Hara jogging toward them, followed some way behind by an older and less fit Detective Inspector Sheehan.

"What is it?" Sadie asked her colleague quickly. O'Hara had found out something.

"A local trawler saw a dinghy heading out two hours ago," he said. Sheehan came up behind him, panting for breath.

"That fits with the timeframe," Sadie said, looking at Harding, her rivalry with the other woman momentarily forgotten. "It has to be Summers."

"What direction was he heading in?" Harding asked. "Is he heading towards another rig?"

"Yes, the Arctic Treader," O'Hara confirmed.

"You were right, Agent Price," Harding said matter-of-factly, surprising Sadie with the acknowledgment. "We need to get back in the air and get to that rig."

75

"I'll stay in touch," the sheriff assured them, "and I'll alert the Arctic Treader."

Harding thanked him before they ran back to the chopper. Even O'Hara threw himself inside without hesitation, as urgent as any of them to get to the rig before the activist did. Sadie knew, for all of their speed, that Summers would already have had time to get aboard the rig. Their chances of intercepting him in time to prevent a murder were slim to none, but they had to try. The fact that as yet no body had been called in was reason for hope.

The chopper was over the ocean in no time, making its way northeast as fast as it was able, the pilot radioing through to the Coast Guard for precise directions to the Arctic Treader. Sadie searched the gray waves underneath her for signs of the dinghy, although the roiling waves would make anything on its surface that size difficult to spot. Summers must be intensely dedicated to risk sailing these waters in so small a craft.

But then Sadie knew from firsthand experience just how dedicated some killers could be.

The rig had just come into view when there was a radio call from the Prudhoe Bay sheriff. The quartet listened in horror as he confirmed what, at heart, they already knew.

A call had come in from the Arctic Treader.

They were too late.

A body had been found hanging from the boom crane.

CHAPTER FIFTEEN

As soon as they touched down the rig manager came running over, a look of both panic and relief on his face.

"You got here really fast," he said. "I've only just called it in."

"We were already at Prudhoe Bay," Sadie said, holding out her hand. As she introduced them, she saw Harding cut her a look and guessed that the other woman thought Sadie was making some kind of point. She hadn't been; she was just still getting used to not being the woman in charge. Once the introductions were over, she stepped back, letting Harding lead the questioning. *Take that, Cooper,* she thought. *No ego here.*

"How long has the body been there?" Harding asked. The rig manager, who had introduced himself as John McIntosh, looked bewildered. He was in shock, Sadie realized, more so than either Mason or Cortez had been, and she wondered just what was different about this body.

"At least a couple of hours," he said. "No one saw it at first, because it's so dark and there was no need for anyone to be up near the boom crane. It was only when we realized that Mr. Joliffe wasn't in his quarters that I figured something was wrong. Then when Marlow, one of the engineers, found him I thought it was suicide, until I saw the side of his head." He shook his head. "I'll show you the body. That's probably the best place to start."

"Who is this Mr. Joliffe?" Harding asked. It was the same question that Sadie had on the edge of her lips.

It wasn't the body that was different. It was the victim. No rig manager was going to refer to his derrick hands as "Mr." anything.

"An executive from the oil company," McIntosh said, and Sadie understood why he was so anxious. Joliffe had been a VIP, and someone had boarded the rig and murdered him right under McIntosh's nose. "Sometimes they send someone over for a day or two to see how everything runs and report back. Making sure they work us to the bone," he said with a curl of his upper lip. Some of the shock was wearing off.

"Can you think of any reason why anyone would want to specifically target him?"

McIntosh thought about it for a moment, his head tipped to one side like a bird, then finally shook his head.

"Nah. It was the first time I had met him, but he seemed a pleasant enough guy, I suppose. Bit flash, but only as you'd expect."

"What about Ed Summers?" Harding asked. "Have you heard of him?"

McIntosh shook his head again, but he frowned as he did so. "I'm not sure…"

"He's an environmental activist," Harding supplied.

"Better known as an ecoterrorist," Sadie cut in, thinking that to describe Summers so benignly was an insult to environmentalists who didn't go around smashing up machinery.

Or murdering people.

At her words McIntosh's expression cleared.

"Yeah, he's the guy who boards the rigs and smashes things up, right? You think he done this?"

"Has he boarded the Arctic Treader before?" Sadie asked.

McIntosh nodded, looking angry now. "Last year. He didn't cause any major damage, thank God, but he made a right mess. He's a murderer now?"

"He's a suspect," Harding said carefully. "We were tracking him when the call about the body—sorry, Mr. Joliffe—came in."

McIntosh looked dazed at that particular piece of information, as though it was all too much for him to process. He took them to the body.

Joliffe had been laid out in the tiny room he had been staying in, on the bunk, and if it wasn't for the red stain on the front of his chest that covered most of his shirt, he could easily have been asleep. Pulling on her gloves while O'Hara took a few photographs of the body, Sadie carefully inspected the wound.

"Gunshot," she said. "He's changed his MO." *Or there's more than one killer*, she thought. This was getting way too complex for comfort. The chances of her and O'Hara getting home any time that day were fading fast.

"The bullet is in the wall there," McIntosh told them, indicating the wall behind a small table in the corner. O'Hara took pictures while Sadie carefully extracted and bagged the bullet.

78

"You didn't hear anything? He must have used a silencer," Sheehan said, answering his own question.

"Not a thing. I don't know how he managed to get away with it," McIntosh said. He sounded angry as much as bewildered now, and Sadie thought of all three of the rig managers that she had met over the last three days, and how it must feel to have their domain invaded like this, and with such ease. As though Summers was no more than a ghost.

He must have practiced this, she thought. Maybe this had been the plan all along, and the vandalism was just a cover. But then, why let himself get caught and imprisoned if that was the case? Sadie looked around the room, imagining Joliffe sitting at the table in the early hours of the morning, and Summers bursting in with his gun.

"He knew Joliffe was here," she said, looking at Harding. "He didn't just go for the first person he found. A derrick hand, an architect, an oil executive...is there a pattern here?"

She was expecting Harding to rebuff her hypothesis, but the British detective looked interested. "Go on, Agent Price," she prompted. "What are you thinking?"

Sadie turned around slowly again, getting her bearings, imagining the distance to the crane, and the long climb to the top. She looked at Joliffe. He wasn't particularly large, but he had some extra weight on him.

"How strong would you say Summers looked? Strong enough to carry Joliffe over his shoulder while he climbed the boom crane? Corpses aren't easy to carry." There was a reason for the term *dead weight*.

"He was no slouch," O'Hara offered. "After all, his record says that he is some kind of martial artist. They're usually a lot stronger than they look."

"Good endurance too," Sheehan offered. "Which he would have needed to get out here on that dinghy, climb up onto the platform, and then drag Joliffe up that crane. And then get back again."

"I wonder where he is now," Harding mused. "He must know that we would pick him up at Prudhoe Bay, and I can't see him heading back to Deadhorse."

Sadie looked over at McIntosh, who was listening intently. "Would any of your crew know Ed Summers in a personal capacity?" she asked. "Are any of them local?"

"A few," the manager said, "but none of my men would have anything to do with this!" He looked horrified as he contemplated the idea.

Sadie wasn't so sure. She had a hunch that Summers wasn't acting entirely alone.

"We need to question your crew," Harding said to the rig manager. "All of them. We'll split into pairs and report back to each other," she added to Sadie, who nodded, already thinking of something else.

Her gut also told her that this wasn't Summers's doing, or at the very least, that he wasn't the main player. Summers, judging by his record and what she had seen of the man, was someone who liked his work to be seen. The vandalism had been brazen, his going to prison part of his whole rhetoric of resistance. This sudden switch to cold-blooded and ruthless murder was all wrong.

But she wasn't going to voice that part just yet. Not with Harding's eyes on her and no proof other than her own gut instinct to back it up.

McIntosh left the room to arrange a space where they could start questioning the crew, looking glad to leave the room with Joliffe's sightless eyes staring at them. Sadie noticed with a twinge of pride that O'Hara wasn't fazed by this body at all. Three in two days and he was a pro.

The quartet were just leaving the room themselves when a sudden shout came from the far side of the platform. They heard feet running and shouts going up. Sadie broke into a run herself, the others close behind her.

On the other side of the rig, a few of the mechanics were hauling something in. Harding looked at McIntosh for clarification. If the rig manager had looked shocked when they arrived, he now looked as though he was about to have a breakdown.

"There's a boat," he said. "Tied to the bottom of the terrace. It looks like a dinghy."

"A dinghy?" Sadie rushed to look over, thinking wildly, *But then Summers must still be aboard.*

At the sight that greeted her as she watched it being hauled in, she realized just how wrong that assumption was.

There was a man lying in the dinghy, not moving, his head at an odd angle to his neck. As the boat came closer Sadie could make out the man's face, confirming what she already knew.

The dead man was Ed Summers.

CHAPTER SIXTEEN

Sadie felt dazed as she sat at a table in the galley with O'Hara, waiting to start interviewing the rest of the crew. Ed Summers's death had shocked them all and thrown the investigation into disarray. Harding seemed to think that Summers was still the culprit but had either been apprehended and killed by one of the derrick hands or had simply fallen from the terrace and broken his neck. Sadie thought both possibilities were unlikely, although if they could find some proof that Summers had simply fallen, that would make the case all but closed. Even a lack of alternative evidence might be enough to close it. Sadie suspected the Brits were as eager to wrap this case up and get home as she was.

But what if they were wrong? If they all left, labeled Summers as the murderer, only for another body to end up swinging on a nearby boom crane? Sadie didn't believe in leaving room for error.

Not to mention the fact that she was already under investigation. An error of that magnitude would dent her otherwise impressive reputation. Lawson would have a field day with that.

The crew members who had found the dinghy, found Joliffe, had been awake and in the vicinity within the timeframe of the murder. Sadie knew that without immediate access to a forensics team and lab they could be missing important details about the murders, but for now they would have to do the best they could.

So far, their investigations that morning had turned up nothing, and Sadie was beginning to feel frustrated. Across the other side of the galley, Harding and Sheehan looked glum too. An atmosphere of frustrated misery pervaded the space.

Next to her, O'Hara stifled a yawn. "I'm not sure I can cope with another night in that motel," he said to Sadie when she looked at him.

"Suck it up, rookie." She grinned, attempting to lighten the mood. O'Hara looked mock offended.

"You're doing pretty good, O'Hara," Sadie told him, amused when the younger agent blushed all the way to the back of his ears. Apart from the airsickness, O'Hara was coping well with what had turned out to be a nightmare of a case, and it seemed her initial worries that he would be a liability had proved to be unfounded. She was glad he was here, if only so she hadn't ended up on her own with the detectives from Scotland Yard.

A derrick hand came over and sat opposite them, a wary expression on his face. He was dark skinned, with a graying beard and a strong, muscled frame. All of the crew were necessarily physically fit, but this guy looked like a prize fighter.

Certainly strong enough to carry Joliffe's body up the boom crane, and to break a neck with his bare hands.

"Mike Miller," he introduced himself, speaking to O'Hara rather than Sadie. "I work the shale shaker."

Sadie made a note of that, remembering the original murder weapon.

"Hi, Mike." Sadie flashed him a smile, retracting it when Miller's eyes swept over her body, lingering on her curves. She eyeballed him but he didn't look at all embarrassed at being caught checking her out; instead he rocked back in his chair and gave her a slight smirk.

"Where were you between six and eight a.m. this morning?" she said coldly. Miller shrugged.

"Asleep until seven," he said. "Then breakfast, and then I started shift at half past seven. I was with the crew the whole time. They can vouch for me."

That's the problem, Sadie thought. Even if something was amiss, she expected the crew would vouch for each other anyway, unless one was carrying a grudge.

The practiced way that Miller answered made Sadie suspect that he had been in trouble with the law before, but that was no big surprise here.

"Tell me about Joliffe," she said. She felt tired. She had a feeling they were going to spend all day interrogating the derrick hands only to leave none the wiser, with an unexpected dead body on their hands.

"Nothing to tell." Miller shrugged. He looked bored. "He didn't say anything to me while he was here. He didn't really speak to anyone other than McIntosh, just wandered around watching us, peering over our shoulders. The executives aren't interested in the likes of us, just how much money we can make them." The resentment dripped from his tongue.

"Sounds like you didn't like him very much," Sadie said, her voice neutral. Miller made a scoffing sound in the back of his throat.

"Why should I? He means nothing to me. But I didn't kill him, if that's what you're asking. Can't say men like him are any big loss to the world though. Summers should concentrate on his lot, not us derrick hands."

Miler's mouth curled in contempt, and Sadie leaned forward slightly in her chair, her senses back on alert.

"You speak about Ed Summers like you know him," she said.

"I know of him," Miller said quickly, too quickly, as though recognizing that he had made a mistake and was trying to rectify it before she or O'Hara noticed. "He's one of those eco warriors. He's caused trouble before."

"Going by your accent, I'm assuming you're a local. Do you know Summers from Deadhorse?" Sadie guessed, knowing that she was right when Miller's cheek twitched.

"I've seen him around," he admitted. "But we don't get ashore much."

"You're not friends?"

Miller laughed. "He thinks we're all gonna be responsible for the apocalypse and the death of the planet. What do you think?"

"I'm more interested in what you think," Sadie said. "You said that Summers should contrate on executives like Joliffe. So you're aware that the first murder he is suspected of is was a derrick hand?"

Miller's expression didn't change, but she saw his eyes go dark with rage.

"We heard that," he said. "Didn't know if it was true."

"'We' being you and your crewmates?"

"Yeah," Miller said, looking wary again. Sadie regarded him for a moment, mulling over the possibilities in her mind. If Summers had been caught aboard the rig after killing Joliffe, by Miller or another of the crew, it was more than possible that there was a physical fight which had ended very badly for the environmental activist. Miller looked as though he could snap a few necks without thinking, his muscles evident even beneath his thick winter gear.

"When was the last time you saw Summers?"

He shrugged again. "Dunno. Months ago."

"You didn't see him this morning? Get up early for a bit of fresh air, maybe?"

Miller glared at her. "Are you deaf, lady? I didn't see anything this morning. I didn't see Joliffe, and I didn't kill Summers."

Sadie met his glare with a cool gaze that she knew would infuriate him more than if she returned his anger. He was riled, and she had no doubt that the man in front of her was capable of the things he felt accused of, but that in itself didn't make him a suspect. Still, she felt that he was one to watch, and Sadie intended to check out Miller carefully for any past record before ruling him out.

The problem, of course, was that plenty of the derrick hands might have a past history of violence. It didn't mean that any of them were guilty of killing Joliffe or Summers. But Sadie still found it hard to believe that Summers was acting alone, or that he could have sneaked aboard three different rigs without being noticed. Sure, he had gotten aboard before, but as soon as he was, he had started vandalizing the place; there had been no real effort to keep his identity or intentions hidden. The levels of stealth that had been required for these operations were something else entirely.

"You can go," Sadie said eventually, once she could see that for all his bravado Miller was starting to squirm. As he walked away, she glanced at O'Hara. "What did you think of Miller?"

"Angry guy," O'Hara commented, looking pleased that Sadie had asked his opinion. "He certainly looked furious at knowing Summers had—we assume—killed another derrick hand. I can see him killing Summers, but the rest? What are his motives?"

"You're echoing my thoughts, O'Hara," Sadie said with a sigh. "I can't see Miller as an environmentalist. Unless we are wrong on that one; distracted by Summers, maybe. It could be partly a grudge against the oil companies, perhaps. They don't always treat their derrick hands well."

"While men like Joliffe are living the high life," O'Hara pointed out.

Sadie nodded. "Maybe we need to start thinking outside the box here."

"You're going to check if Miller has a record?"

"I'm going to check all of them," Sadie confirmed. "But Miller is at the top of my list, sure. The fact that he's a local and could have known Summers personally is interesting. Perhaps they had different motives, but the same ends? They could have agreed to work together."

"With Miller doing the killings?" O'Hara suggested. "He seems a more likely candidate than Eco Ed, martial artist or not."

Sadie laughed quietly at the moniker that O'Hara had given Summers. "I would agree, but then what about the first derrick hand?

That was our motive for Miller killing Summers." She shook her head, feeling exasperated with this case once again. "It's always good to consider different scenarios, but I feel as though we're getting further away with every potential lead, not closer. While whoever is responsible is running rings around us. Every time we turn our backs, another body appears. Two, this time."

O'Hara looked disappointed at her words, and Sadie considered what this case might mean for O'Hara. It was the first time he had been sent out of jurisdiction, and he had ended up partnered with her, a BAU specialist and, whether she liked it or not, something of a local hero, and working with Scotland Yard. If they could wrap this up, it would look great for his career, as well as giving him a much-needed confidence boost.

"We'll get him," Sadie said, with more confidence that she actually felt. "And while I have the chance to tell you, I'm enjoying working with you, O'Hara. You have the makings of a fine agent."

O'Hara looked as though all his Christmases had come at once, but whatever he was about to say in response was lost as a small, wiry older man with a sparse gray beard sat down opposite them. The next crew member to be questioned.

Sadie gave him a nod, snapping back into interrogation mode and trying not to let her tiredness show.

"Alan McMahon," the man introduced himself. "I've been working these rigs for nearly thirty years," he said with the pride evident in his voice, "and I can tell you I've never known anything like this before. Accidents, suicides, even a near beating to death once, but this? Not good. It's like something evil blew in on the north wind." He gave a superstitious shudder that seemed overly exaggerated to Sadie, which immediately made her suspicious. Maybe McMahon was just a theatrical guy, or maybe he was overplaying his fright.

They ran through the same questions that they had with all of the crew, only to get the same answers. He hadn't seen anything, hadn't heard anything, and didn't know why anyone would want to kill either Joliffe or the activist.

"Mind you," he said, "those environmentalists are dangerous, I've always said that. That sooner or later they always go too far. Serves the bastard right if he broke his neck falling off the platform if you ask me. Nothing but a troublemaker."

"Have you ever met Mr. Summers personally?"

85

McMahon shook his head. "No, but I don't need to. I've met enough of them over the years, and they're deluded, the lot of them. I've always said it. They target us as if all the world's problems are our fault. I mean, we all know now that fossil fuels ain't too good for ol' Mother Earth, but what else do they suggest we do? Let people freeze to death? Not much chance of solar panels up here." He laughed at his own joke, showing browning, broken teeth.

"Murder seems a step up from the usual types of protest though," O'Hara cut in. The old man turned his beady eyes onto the young agent.

"It does, doesn't it?" he agreed.

Then he clammed up, seeming to have nothing more to say.

Perhaps he thought he had said too much.

Sadie had just told him he could go and was watching him walk away, both relieved that he was the last crew member they had to question and frustrated that they had found out nothing concrete, when McMahon suddenly rushed back to their table. He leaned into them, his voice barely above a whisper.

"I did see another boat," he said. "Not too far from the rig, this morning when we were getting Joliffe down. I didn't think much of it at first, you do see the little fishing boats out here from time to time. But thinking about it now…maybe the activist guy wasn't alone? I mean, he was a pretty fat guy, ol' Joliffe."

Sadie and O'Hara exchanged a glance, and Sadie felt a fizz of anticipation in her stomach. She almost wanted to hug McMahon.

"Can you describe it? Or anyone in it?" she asked, hiding her excitement. After all, it could be nothing.

Instinct, though, told her this was important.

"Not really. It was dark as hell. But it was a nice little cruiser, not like the dinghy we found the guy in."

"Thank you." Sadie stood up and caught Harding's eye from across the room. The British detectives were also finished with questioning and looked as frustrated as she and O'Hara. Sadie jerked her head to indicate that she had something to say and saw the same sharp interest glint in Harding's eyes.

Sadie knew that look. The hunt was on.

*

86

As the helicopter took off from the rig's helipad, Sadie called through for the Coast Guard at Prudhoe Bay, asking for him to track details of any vessel that had reached port that day. As she ended the call, she looked around at the quartet inside the chopper.

The news of a possible second vessel involved in the killings had reinvigorated them, and even O'Hara seemed less bothered by his airsickness than at any other point over the last two days. They eagerly shared information on the questioning of the crew members, although Harding and Sheehan had even less to report.

"Well, we have a list of crew members who we particularly want to check for priors, including Mr. Miller," Harding said, reviewing her notes and adding the information that Sadie had given her. "He's the only one who admitted to knowing Summers on anything approaching a personal level, so he's certainly worthy of further consideration. Although I doubt a derrick hand is involved, especially now that we have the possibility of a second boat. Good work, Agents."

She said the last as though she was praising children, Sadie thought, but for once she let it slide. She was getting used to Harding and was just glad that she wasn't Sheehan and didn't have to work with her daily.

"That's if the second vessel has anything to do with this," Sadie said, urging caution even though she was excited herself about this latest lead. "But it seems like too much of a coincidence to not be related. The Coast Guard should be able to tell us more."

O'Hara was looking thoughtful. "The way McMahon told us though," he said slowly, "it seemed odd, don't you think? You already asked him if he had seen anything else. I didn't buy the way it just suddenly occurred to him."

"Me neither," Sadie agreed, impressed with O'Hara's assessment of McMahon, "but he seemed to have a bit of a flair for the theatrical. He might have just wanted to seem important. It isn't that unusual, is it, a boat on the waters? But the way he told us; he had obviously been thinking about what it might mean."

Harding was listening to her intently. "Or perhaps he wasn't sure if he wanted to tell us," she said.

"Maybe he knew damn well who it was and was just messing us about," Sheehan growled. Sadie was getting the impression that the gruff Northerner had well and truly had enough and just wanted to go home. "He's probably involved as well," he added cynically. "That's why we're getting nowhere. They're all covering up for each other."

Harding glanced at him. "There's no need for conspiracy theories, Inspector," she sniffed. Sheehan raised a bushy eyebrow at her.

"This is a man's world out here ma'am," he said bluntly. "With respect, not an area you'd know about. They will all cover for each other, mark my words."

Harding looked as though she wanted to slap Sheehan for his comment and Sadie looked away discreetly, staring out of the window. O'Hara caught her eye, looking as though he was about to start laughing.

The atmosphere in the chopper was tangibly awkward, and Sadie was glad when her radio went off.

"Prudhoe Bay," she said, snatching it up, eager for information on the as yet still mysterious second boat.

It was the sheriff, not the Coast Guard.

"Agent Price. I've got the information you wanted," he said, sounding none too pleased. Sadie wondered what had happened.

"There have been boats coming into port?" she asked eagerly, praying it wouldn't just turn out to be a licensed fishing boat.

"Just the one," he said, and then fell silent as though he was reluctant to share the information.

"And the details?" Sadie said impatiently.

"They won't be any use to you," the sheriff said. "Not relevant, really."

"We'll be the judge of that, Sheriff," Sadie snapped. The other detectives' eyes bored into her as they listened to her end of the conversation, as impatient for the information as she was. "Could you tell me who and what it was, please?"

The sheriff gave a frustrated sigh. "A private launch," he said reluctantly. "Belongs to a Prudhoe local named Peter Tenby, but no one calls him that. Half the town won't even know his real name, I'm betting. We call him the Birdman. He uses his boat to clean up after all the oil spills we get. He rescues the birds, see. From fishermen's nets as well, but it's the oil spills that do the most damage, as you can imagine. He's tireless. And a nice guy. Bit of a local hero, in fact."

"Have you detained him for questioning?" Sadie asked, already knowing what the answer was going to be.

"Of course not," the Prudhoe Bay sheriff said, sounding shocked. "It's Birdman. He's never harmed anyone in his life. He won't have anything to do with this."

"We need to talk to him," Sadie insisted. "What's his address?"

The sheriff sighed heavily before he gave it to her. "But you'll find him in the tavern," he said. "Although you won't make friends around here, questioning locals like this. We're not killers, Agent, and especially not our Birdman."

Too annoyed to argue, Sadie replaced her radio and relayed the information to the others, trying to curb her anger at the sheriff. If Birdman had anything to do with this, then their main suspect had just been allowed to walk free.

"The local sheriffs aren't particularly helpful, are they?" Harding said coolly. They were all still angry at how easily Ed Summers had gotten away, and now this.

"Even if he's right," O'Hara said, "we still need to question him. If he was in the vicinity, then he could have seen something."

"He might have done a lot more than seen something," Sadie agreed. "He's got the perfect cover if nobody around here suspects him and are used to seeing him out on the Beaufort, and he's got the motive too. Another environmentalist, and one with a local—and therefore more personal—passion. He has every reason to hate the rigs and everyone who works on them if he spends his time rescuing the animals they've harmed."

The quartet nodded at each other in unison.

It was time to find the Birdman.

CHAPTER SEVENTEEN

As they approached the Prudhoe Bay tavern, Sadie was still shaking her head at the local sheriff's attitude toward the Birdman. As far as Sadie was concerned, everyone was a suspect. Local hero or not. She had learned the hard way over the years to never rule out anyone even peripherally connected with a case.

For once, she and Harding seemed to be on the same page, as Harding fell into step beside her, tutting loudly.

"The local sheriffs around here seem to be remarkably short-sighted," she said in her cut-glass accent. "How he didn't think to detain this bird person for questioning is beyond me."

"My thoughts exactly," Sadie responded, the exasperation showing in her voice. There was music coming from the tavern, and raucous laughter. Entering a busy bar to interrogate a local hero wasn't going to go down well with a bunch of drunken townies and would make their job harder than it needed to be.

"He seemed to think the pigeon man, or whatever he called him, was beyond suspicion," Harding said incredulously. "No one is beyond suspicion, wouldn't you say, Agent Price?"

"No one likes to think that someone that they like or respect could be guilty of murder," Sadie replied. "We think of murderers—especially multiple and serial killers—as monsters. Not like regular people; inhuman, somehow. But we both know that's never the case. Sometimes it's the quiet loner or guy with a record, sure, but more often than not it's the person you least expect. Someone's father, husband, brother…They might lead a perfectly normal life otherwise." She thought of the Mangler and suppressed a shudder, not wanting Harding to see and comment on her discomfiture.

Instead, Harding was looking at her with an expression that Sadie almost thought was admiration. "It can't be easy, your job," she said. "A lot of mine is desk work, these days. But you're right on the ground here, aren't you? Trying to get into these killers' heads."

"Trust me, I would rather stay out of them," Sadie said with a sigh.

"This case is quite particularly baffling, don't you think?" Sadie was surprised at the tremor of uncertainty in the other woman's words, For the first time she realized that Detective Superintendent Harding was as frustrated and doubtful about these murders as she was.

"Yes," Sadie said honestly. "There seem to be so many leads that never actually lead anywhere, and every time we think we're getting somewhere another body turns up. It's been the longest two days I've had in a while."

"Me, too," Harding said with a genuine smile that softened her features considerably. In the light from the tavern's window, she looked really quite attractive. Sadie wondered if the British detective ever got the chance to let her hair down. Being a female heading up a Scotland Yard division couldn't be easy.

"You're a good detective, Agent Price," Harding went on as they approached the doorway. Sadie blinked, wondering if she had heard the woman correctly, went Harding went on. "I must apologize if I have been somewhat standoffish. I'm not used to dealing with other women being in charge. I suppose I've always seen them as rivals, really. It wasn't easy, getting to my rank in London, you know."

Sadie opened and shut her mouth, momentarily at a loss for what to say. Harding's apology and confession had completely blindsided her. She wanted to thank her and say sorry too, but then they were right outside the tavern and Sheehan and O'Hara, just ahead of them, were walking inside. The smell of stale beer and tobacco reached them as the door swung open and Harding sniffed disapprovingly, back to her usual self. Sadie smiled as she followed them inside.

The tavern was small, dingy, and crowded. It reminded her of Caz's saloon back home, except that it didn't feel as welcoming, and the interior décor was more tattered and the floor sticky under her boots. Caz would have died before she would let her establishment get this filthy.

As the quartet approached the bar, the loud chatter quieted to a suspicious murmur as heads turned to look at them. The bartender, a large, almost obese man with a missing front tooth, was the only person who seemed relatively pleased to see them, flashing them what was meant to be a welcoming grin but looked more like a grimace, Sadie thought, trying not to notice his chins wobbling as he leaned toward them.

"What can I get you fine folks?"

"We're not here for a drink. We're looking for a man who goes by the name of Birdman," Sadie said quickly, before Harding could mangle the man's moniker.

The smile vanished from the bartender's face, and the small crowd of men at the bar, who had been whispering among themselves as they approached, fell silent.

"What do you want with him?" The bartender no longer sounded welcoming. When Sadie introduced herself and the others, his smile turned into an outright glare.

"We just need to ask your man a few questions," Sheehan said in his Northern English growl. The bartender looked curious and less menacing at his accent.

"You've come all the way from England? Well, that warrants a drink on us. But what do you want to question the Birdman about?"

"I can ask them myself, Eddie, thanks," a reedy voice came from the small crowd at the bar. A small, wiry man with a hooked nose and greasy hair pushed through the crowd and eyed them warily.

The Birdman. He looked at Sadie and she noticed his eyes were a startling green. "What do you want with me?" he asked. There was no malice in his voice.

Harding didn't attempt to jump in, so Sadie took the lead. "We need to ask you a few questions about your boat," she said. "In private."

A taller man, thickset and with arms covered in crude tattoos, pushed his way forward, standing next to the Birdman with his arms folded. He glowered at Sadie, and then at each of the others, clearly distrustful of them and protective of his friend. The Birdman was well loved.

Enough for them all to cover for him?

"Why in private?" the tattooed man challenged. "Four Feds to one man? That sounds like police harassment to me. He needs a lawyer."

"Yeah," came another voice, from across the tavern this time. "Leave him alone."

"He's done nothing wrong," another one yelled.

"And how would you know that," Harding asked, turning her head elegantly in the direction of the last voice, "if we can't question him?"

There was a momentary silence at Harding's cool, upper-class voice and her aura of being unruffled and in charge. Even the tattooed friend of the Birdman looked impressed.

92

The silence didn't last long. Eddie leaned over his bar toward them. "I don't want any trouble in my tavern," he warned. "Police or no police."

"If we could step outside for a moment?" Harding asked the Birdman. The man looked unsure, and Sadie didn't blame him. In here, with a whole crowd of guys who clearly supported him regardless of what he might have done, he had the upper hand.

"Birdman hasn't done nothing," Tattoo Guy growled. "If he had, you would just arrest him."

Sadie sighed, realizing they were unlikely to get anywhere in this situation. Even so, she addressed the Birdman calmly, ignoring his overprotective friend.

"We just need to know where you have just returned from," she said, her voice quiet so the whole tavern couldn't hear. When the man answered, however, he raised his voice as though ensuring all the avidly listening locals could hear.

"What do you mean, where have I just come from?" he said, echoing her question. He looked at Eddie the bartender. "I've been here since this morning, haven't I, Eddie?"

"That's right," Eddie said without a pause. "Been here all day. Nothing like a few whiskeys to warm you in this weather."

Sadie raised an eyebrow. Birdman seemed stone cold sober to her, unlike his friend whose eyes were slightly unfocused, as was the small crowd behind them. If Birdman had been drinking with them all day, then he was either a very slow drinker or a highly accomplished one.

"That's right," a voice shouted from the back of the tavern. "I've been here all day too. Birdman hasn't been anywhere."

"Me too," another one yelled. "I can vouch for him."

As Sadie was expecting, the man with the tattoos spoke next. "He's been with us all day. I've been right next to him. How much more proof do you need?"

Sadie met his eyes, and then Eddie's, and then swept her gaze around the tavern. "This is a murder investigation," she told them. The tavern fell deathly silent again as this news was processed. "If you're willing to vouch for him, I'll need to take names and addresses. Are you all okay with that?"

"Because if it turns out you're lying," O'Hara spoke up behind her, "I'll haul all your asses in for obstructing the law."

There was a tense silence. Birdman, Sadie noticed, looked scared now, taking a step back so he was once again surrounded by his friends.

93

He looked at Eddie, and Sadie saw the bartender give the smaller man a nod.

"Hell, yeah, you can take my details," Eddie said. "I live right here, and my name is above the door. And Birdman has been here all day, with us."

The look of relief on Birdman's face was palpable.

"Mine too," Tattoo Guy spoke up, putting a friendly arm around Birdman's shoulders. "Lex Guthrie. I live just over the road, cabin with the blue door."

"Johnny Smith," the man behind him said. "I live next door."

Sadie met Harding's gaze and saw her frustration matched in the woman's eyes. "Let's go around and take down names and addresses of everyone who can vouch for Birdman here," she said. "Then we'll reconvene outside."

Sadie nodded and walked to the back of the tavern where the voices had been coming from, O'Hara following behind her, while Harding and Sheehan stayed at the bar to take the names of Birdman's immediate crowd of friends.

People turned their backs as Sadie and O'Hara approached, apart from two men who came forward. The ones who had been shouting, Sadie guessed.

"Tyler Morley. Cottage down at the wharf," the first one said, sounding bored. His friend, a wry old man with a white beard, gave them a toothless grin. "Amos," he said. "I live here, above the tavern. I'm Eddie's dad."

Sadie struggled to find a resemblance.

"You won't make any friends here, questioning Birdie," Amos went on. "He's a good Christian guy, one of those selfless ones you hear about. A saint, almost. Spends all his time rescuing and cleaning up baby birds, you know that? It's his passion, what he lives for. And you're coming in here asking him questions about murders." The old man tutted.

"That's my job," Sadie said without apology. "And I find it hard to believe half of Prudhoe Bay's working-age men are sitting here in the tavern all day."

That wasn't quite true, because Sadie knew that unemployment was often rife in places like this, but she wanted to see Amos's response. The old man simply shrugged. "They're mostly fishermen in here. There's not much else going unless you want to work the rigs. And

94

with the winds up, there's not been many boats out today. Not the right season either."

"I see. Thank you for your time." Sadie and O'Hara went back outside. After the stale smell of the tavern, she almost welcomed the sub-zero temperatures even as she pulled her fur-lined hood and scarf back around her face.

"Did you believe him? Amos?" O'Hara asked.

"It's plausible about the fishermen being in the tavern all day, sure. But do I believe the Birdman was? No. Did you see the way he and the bartender looked at each other? It was as though he was asking him to cover up for him. But we can't prove he wasn't there, not with all of those alibis. It could take a whole other day just to check them out."

"But we didn't ask him about his boat," O'Hara said, sounding confused. "Someone took his boat out. If it wasn't him, he needs to know someone has used it."

"You're right," Sadie said. "But I don't want that information all around the tavern, so that if anyone in there knows anything, they can cook up a story between them. We need to speak to the Birdman on his own. We can wait until he comes out."

O'Hara looked disappointed. Sadie didn't blame him. She was longing for sleep, even if it was in some dingy motel.

"Good call, Agent Price," Harding's voice came from behind them as she and Sheehan exited the tavern. "But I think I may have a better idea."

"Oh?" Sadie asked, trying to sound friendly. The other woman's apology had touched her, and she didn't want the frostiness between them to resume. Besides which, Harding hadn't made superintendent without knowing how to do her job.

"Birdman's boat came back to its usual anchor, the sheriff said. If we can persuade him to give us a warrant to search it—and I'm sure reminding him that the British Embassy will be getting involved if he doesn't cooperate will help—then we might be able to track where the boat has been, depending on what navigation the boat has onboard."

Sadie nodded, annoyed that she hadn't thought of that. Of course, she would have wanted to search the boat, but GPS tracking hadn't occurred to her. This wasn't the sort of case she was used to.

And she hated feeling out of her depth.

"What difference will it make, though?" O'Hara asked, sounding confused. "We know the boat was out there, but he's got an alibi for not being on it."

"All we know right now for certain," Sadie said patiently, "is that the boat was out on the sea at the time of the killings, potentially. We don't know if it was anywhere near the Arctic Treader. It's always possible that the Birdman took the boat out elsewhere, but freaked out when the four of us walked in. Some people are so jumpy around law enforcement they will lie even when they're innocent."

"Yes," Harding continued. "If we discover the boat was nowhere near the Arctic Treader, we know we don't need to pursue this any further. If it was, then we either break his alibi or we find out who stole the boat. Either way it would be a solid lead."

"If it wasn't," Sheehan cut in, his voice hoarse. "Then we're back to bloody square one. I've had enough of this cold," he added. "We need to get this sorted before my toes fall off."

Harding rolled her eyes at her partner as Sadie called the Prudhoe Bay sheriff. As Harding had predicted, he sounded reluctant to give them a warrant for the Birdman's boat.

"It's vital that we get on that boat," Sadie insisted. "If you won't grant us the warrant, I'll have to go over your head. And it isn't me who is in charge of this…" She let the sentence linger unfinished, but the sheriff picked up on her threat of international involvement and grunted down the phone.

"Okay, Agent, give me an hour. I'll meet you there. I was about to sit in front of the fire with my wife," he grumbled as he ended the call.

Sadie nodded at the others.

"We're on," she said. "Let's go."

They headed back toward the wharf, moving quickly against the cold. It was nighttime now and the air was bitter. Sadie hoped the Birdman's boat could tell them what they needed to know. Her adrenaline started to rise, taking over from her earlier frustration. Instinct told her that, after a series of dead ends, they were getting close.

It was a race against time, she felt that keenly.

Because although there were many things they still didn't know about this case, there was one thing that Sadie knew for certain.

This killer was reckless for his own safety. He had killed under the noses of dozens of men on the rigs and kept killing even when he must surely have known that they were on his tail. Whatever his motive and intentions were, they were bigger than him. He must know that sooner or later, if he kept killing, he would get caught.

And he would keep killing until he did.

96

They had to stop him.
Tonight.

CHAPTER EIGHTEEN

Sadie ran her eyes over the Birdman's cabin cruiser. It was loaded with tarp and what looked to be various detergents and cleaning supplies, which fit with what they had been told about him.

It also, she knew, made for an incredibly good motive for Birdman being out on the Beaufort at all hours and in all weather. It was a good boat too, and certainly better for large-scale operations than Ed Summers's dinghy, while still being small enough to not be easily seen from the rigs in the dark.

It was dark now; the North Alaskan dark of night that seemed to suck even the memory of light into it. Sadie's flashlight lit up a line of sight in front of her, but everything either side was lost in the blackness. She could see the flashlights of the others sweeping over the deck of Birdman's cruiser.

"I'll look for the GPS system," Harding said, next to her. She was close enough that Sadie could hear the woman breathing, but she couldn't see her. Sadie had thought she was used to Alaskan winters and the dark that went on and on, but the north was something else entirely.

"I'll look around, see what we can find. O'Hara?"

"I'm here," O'Hara said from behind her, so close that he made her jump.

The four made their way onto the boat, being careful not to slip on the deck where water from the sea had frozen into a thin sheen of ice on the surface. Sheehan groaned.

"I've never known cold like this," he grumbled. "My very bones are frozen."

"It makes England seem positively tropical," Harding agreed.

Sadie smiled to herself as she made her way to the end of the boat, O'Hara next to her. Their flashlights swept the piles of tarp. A tangle of ropes covered one area, including, she noticed with a jolt of interest, a variety of knots.

"O'Hara, look," she said, training the beam of her light onto them. "Let's see if there's a French bowline in among those."

They crouched down next to each other, rummaging through the knots.

"Do you think it really could be this guy?" O'Hara asked. Sadie thought about it for a moment. Logic said that everything currently pointed toward the local man, from his ability to get around, obvious nautical skills, and his passion for wildlife supplying him with a motive. She also didn't believe his alibi for one moment, even if that was currently difficult to prove.

The man's physique, however, gave her pause. He was wiry, and no doubt stronger than he looked, but he was still small and lean. She had no doubt he could scale a rig and climb up and down a boom tower crane in no time, but could he do that with a body over his shoulder? And could he really have broken Ed Summers's neck? Perhaps if he had caught him by surprise…but it took a lot of strength and skill to snap someone's neck, and as far as the Prudhoe sheriff had told them, there was nothing in the Birdman's background to suggest that he had those skills.

Still, people could surprise you in their ability to perform seemingly impossible feats, she thought, and that was as true of villains as it was of heroes. Perhaps the Birdman had just had enough of years of cleaning up after spills from the rigs and seeing the damage that could be caused by them, and that had tipped him over the edge. He could have been preparing for this for a long time, scoping out the rigs and working out the right time to strike. No one would have thought anything about him being out on the water; in fact, that was exactly where they would expect him to be.

Hiding in plain sight.

But that didn't explain where Summers had come in. They could have been working together; after all, they were both local environmental activists and were likely to know one another. But then why kill Summers? Or perhaps the other man really had just fallen from the rig in their haste to get off.

And why take both boats?

Sadie sighed, not knowing how to answer O'Hara.

"I don't know," she said finally, honestly. "Hopefully Harding can get into the GPS, and that will either rule him out or implicate him. Then we'll have something to go on. At the moment, he's got an alibi which, while I don't buy it for a moment, we can't disprove unless we can definitively locate him elsewhere."

"We can't go back to Anchorage without solving this," O'Hara said, sounding nervous. "Golightly wouldn't be happy."

Sadie smiled to herself in the darkness. O'Hara was still young enough and eager to please enough that he was frightened of what Golightly would say.

"We'll solve it," she said firmly, though she had to wonder who she was trying to reassure more; O'Hara or herself.

She could see O'Hara's hands in the flashlight, rummaging through the ropes. "I've found something," he said, pulling a length of knotted rope out of the tangle. "Look at this."

Sadie shone her flashlight on it and whistled under her breath. The knot matched the ones found around the necks of the victims as their bodies hung from the boom tower cranes. She whistled under her breath.

"It's a French bowline. Well spotted," she said. She couldn't see his face but could somehow sense O'Hara smile in the darkness.

"Let's go and show Harding," she said. She nearly slipped as she got to her feet, falling into O'Hara, who managed to catch her by the elbow, hauling her to her feet.

"Thanks," she said, and then, when O'Hara didn't move, "You can let go of my arm now."

"Oh, yes, right, sorry." O'Hara let go so rapidly that he almost slipped instead. Shaking her head, Sadie made her way carefully over to the other side of the boat. O'Hara would be a good agent, she was sure of it, but he needed to get over his nerves.

"Agent O'Hara found a French bowline," she told the two British officers as she approached. They examined it, nodding as they took in the intricate pattern of the knotted rope.

"Yes, it definitely is," Harding said thoughtfully. "So, we know that the suspect could have knotted those ropes."

"But could he have carried the bodies all the way up those crane towers by himself?" Sheehan asked, echoing Sadie's own thoughts.

"We'll soon find out," Harding said, peering at the GPS and tapping furiously. She stared at the screen, the angular lines of her face making her look almost otherworldly in the light of the three flashlights now trained on her. She pressed another button and then a triumphant smile spread across her face.

"Here we are," she said. She read out the coordinates as the cruiser's last journey flashed up on the screen. "He was out by the Arctic Treader," she said, excitement sounding in her voice.

"What time?" Sadie asked, impatient as Harding started pressing buttons again.

"Early this morning," Harding said, glancing around at them. "We've got him. I'll take the GPS and we can go back and get details for the times of the other two murders, but we've got enough to go and arrest him right now for the murder of Joliffe—and we can question him about Summers's unfortunate accident."

"What if he holds to his alibi?" O'Hara asked. "I don't think those guys in the tavern are going to crumble, no matter how much evidence against the Birdman we've got. In fact, they'll probably close ranks even tighter."

Sadie nodded, agreeing with O'Hara. "Let me lead the questioning," she said to Harding.

The older woman looked uncertain. "I'm the superior rank here," she said.

"I know," Sadie said, trying to sound placating rather than frustrated, "but I'm Alaskan. I grew up around local men, fishermen and hunters and wildlife experts. I know how to talk to men like Birdman. Let me try," she offered, "and if I'm not getting anywhere then I'll gladly let you take over."

There was an awkward silence while Harding took her time contemplating Sadie's suggestion. Finally, she nodded.

"Very well, Agent Price," she said. "You do that. But if you get nowhere within half an hour, I'll be taking over. We all want to get home, I'm sure."

In the flashlight Sadie saw Sheehan glance at his partner in surprise, and she guessed he was rarely allowed to lead on an investigation.

"Thank you," Sadie said, meaning it.

As they made their way off the boat, ready to walk back up to the tavern and arrest the Birdman, Sadie still felt unsure about the whole thing, even though they now had better leads and more evidence than since they had started investigating. Something was still niggling at her, telling her that they had missed something.

Something important.

But the more she went over and over things in her head, the less she could see where that might be. Everything pointed to Birdman and Ed Summers working together. Although unless Birdman confessed, they might not ever find out what had happened to Summers. Or just why he had broken out of the Deadhorse sheriff's jail to go racing toward the Arctic Treader and put himself straight back in the way of arrest.

Perhaps Birdman needed Summers to carry the bodies, and that was the answer; no extra strength was needed because there were two murderers.

Yet something told Sadie that wasn't quite right, either.

Maybe it didn't matter. As long as they could deliver a culprit, preferably with a signed and sealed confession, and keep the various oil conglomerates happy, they could, as Harding had said, all just go home. But Sadie wasn't a detective to leave any stone unturned.

Whatever it is, it will come out in questioning, she thought. *As long as we don't lose the suspect this time.*

They reached the tavern, and Harding hung back, motioning for Sadie to do the honors. "You can arrest him, Agent, as you're going to start the questioning," she said graciously, as though conferring a great honor. Sadie just nodded at her, no longer distracted by the ambivalent working relationship between herself and Harding. They were closing in on this case and she wanted to get it locked down and ensure that no more bodies were destined to be hung from towers on the oil rigs in the Beaufort Sea.

"Come on then," she said, walking inside the tavern and sounding more certain than she felt. "Let's go and arrest our murderer."

CHAPTER NINETEEN

Sadie, O'Hara, and the British detectives walked back into the same tavern they had left an hour before to feel hostile stares on them.

"Back again?" someone called from a gloomy corner of the bar.

"Can't keep away," the tattooed man from earlier grumbled, turning his back to them. There was no sign of the Birdman.

The bartender sighed as Sadie approached.

"Going to buy anything this time?"

"Sorry, no," Sadie said curtly. "We really do need to speak to Birdman. New evidence has come to light."

At her words there was a hushed silence in the smoky tavern, and she could feel every eye in the place on her. Sadie was hard to intimidate, but she found herself for once feeling glad that she hadn't walked in there alone. She knew from experience that the more rural parts of Alaska could be insular places, distrustful of and even hostile toward outsiders.

Even more so when they came with a federal badge.

"You're out of luck," the bartender said, picking up a glass and starting to polish it. "He's already left. Not long after you guys. Sorry." He sounded the exact opposite of apologetic.

Sadie gritted her teeth. "Do you know where he went?"

The bartender shrugged. "Down to his boat, I think."

Sadie turned on her heel and left without saying goodbye. Outside, the quartet looked at each other in frustration.

"He could have seen us searching his boat," Sadie said. "Which means he could have gone straight on the run. He must know we would check the GPS and find out that he was lying about not being out on the boat today."

"He could still be around," Sheehan said. "Let's get down there."

They were already jogging down to the wharf as he spoke.

"Get the sheriff back out," Harding said as they ran, her breath curling in the bitter air. "And I don't care how late it is or how much he likes this bird fellow. We need his help; he knows the area and where Tenby is most likely to go."

Sadie nodded, agreeing with her, although she wondered if the sheriff was likely to be more of a hindrance than a help. Still, Harding was right. They would be running around in the dark blind on their own and Sadie doubted that the Birdman would have simply gone back to his home in the boondocks. Plus, the sheriff had a jeep that they could use. No one needed to be outside for too long in these temperatures.

She was surprised when they reached the wharf to find the Birdman's cruiser still in its sloop, exactly as they had left it, with no sign of the Birdman himself.

"I was expecting him to make a run for it on his boat," Harding said, sounding as though she wasn't sure whether to be confused or relieved.

"Perhaps he's going to brazen it out," Sheehan suggested. "He does have an alibi that we might struggle to crack."

"Sadie will crack it," O'Hara offered, sounding so entirely convinced of that fact that Sadie had to stop herself from blushing, especially when Harding turned a cool eye on her.

"It's rather nice to see that your junior agents have such faith in you, Special Agent Price. Your reputation must require quite some living up to."

You have no idea, Sadie thought, grateful to be saved from answering by the arrival of the Prudhoe Bay sheriff, rumbling through the ice and snow in his large Jeep. He jumped out, bundling his scarf around his face. He looked less than happy.

"Birdman's boat's still here then," he said, as if that proved the man's innocence.

"We need to question him immediately," Harding said. "Can you take us to his residence, please?"

"Question him or arrest him?" the sheriff challenged, looking as though he had no intention of taking them anywhere.

"Arrest him," Sadie said shortly, "because we have enough evidence to show he was out on the water today, right next to the Arctic Treader within the likely timeframe of the murders, and that he—and half of Prudhoe's residents—has lied about it. I don't care how popular he is, we need to find him."

"And I'm sure," Harding said in saccharine tones when the sheriff looked as though he was going to argue with Sadie, "that you don't want to be solely responsible for holding up an international investigation?"

104

The sheriff looked mutinously from Sadie to Harding, then as Harding's words sank in his shoulders slumped.

"Come on then," he said with a heavy sigh, climbing back into his Jeep. The quartet piled in after him, with Harding and Sheehan in the front and Sadie and O'Hara in the back. As the sheriff pulled off, Sadie stared out across the wharf, watching the full disc of the moon glinting on the surface of the Beaufort Sea in the distance. There was a cold, almost desolate beauty to the place, and she shuddered as she had a sudden visual image of the first body, swinging in the freezing air from the crane, its features frozen in terror.

They had to stop it from happening again. None of these men deserved to die, up here in the loneliest corners of the world.

The sheriff headed out toward the boondocks, driving too fast along the winding, rocky road. If it could be called a road at all. Sadie found herself flung practically onto O'Hara's lap as they were thrown from side to side in the back of the Jeep.

"Sorry." She winced in sympathy as she accidentally landed an elbow into his ribs.

"I'm sure he's doing it on purpose," O'Hara murmured. "He's not at all happy about us questioning is friend."

"You're telling me," Sadie murmured sarcastically, gripping the edges of her seat. The sheriff's insistence that the Birdman had nothing to do with this bothered her. The Prudhoe Bay sheriff wouldn't be the first law enforcement official to be blinded by personal bias, whether positive or negative, but until this he hadn't struck Sadie as someone who would make those decisions lightly. He seemed to really believe that the Birdman was innocent, and that had to count for something.

Unless he was deliberately covering up for the man, just as the tavern-goers seemed to be only too happy to. He must be loved to be able to claim this much loyalty. Would such a guy really be a cold-blooded murderer?

But then, Sadie had brought down plenty of murderers who had turned out to be people that no one would suspect There was no reason to think that the Birdman was any different.

She stared out the window again, seeing nothing except the narrow stretches of landscape that were picked out by the Jeep's headlights. She could see from them that they were driving now alongside a steep embankment, just inches away from the drop. She wished the sheriff would slow down and told herself that he was a local and probably knew every last inch of this road.

105

Even so, she gripped the edges of the seat that little bit tighter.

She was preparing herself mentally to question the suspect when something in the headlights suddenly caught her eye and she sat straight up in her seat.

"Stop!" she yelled. "There's been a crash."

The sheriff slammed the brakes on so abruptly that they were all jolted harshly forward and the Jeep skidded on the ice, coming to a stop just before they plunged down the side of the embankment. Sadie wasn't surprised to find her legs shaking as she stepped out of the Jeep.

The sheriff turned on his flashlight, picking up the scene Sadie had spotted outside the window. A vehicle had crashed at the bottom of the embankment, tipping onto its side in the snow, half mangled by the pine tree it had careered into.

"Jesus Christ," the sheriff swore. "That's Birdman's truck."

Sadie half ran, half skidded down the embankment, the others close behind her. She had nearly reached the truck when she tripped over something soft and heavy at her feet.

As she stepped back and shone her flashlight down in front of her, she retched as she saw what she had so nearly fallen over.

It was a man's body, his head and torso mangled by impact, ruby red blood spilling out across the frozen tundra.

"Looks like he went straight through the windshield," Sheehan said.

"Poor bastard," the sheriff groaned, sounding devastated.

They wouldn't be questioning the Birdman tonight.

Or ever.

He lay dead at Sadie's feet.

CHAPTER TWENTY

Sadie kept an eye on O'Hara as the local doctor, doubling up as a medical examiner, carefully examined the Birdman's body back at the tiny Prudhoe Bay station. His torso and face were pretty badly mangled, and O'Hara was looking decidedly green. It made Sadie remember just how much of a rookie O'Hara was, fresh from Quantico. Next to him, Sheehan and Harding were unfazed. Sadie suspected that, like herself, they had seen much worse.

She couldn't remember what it was like to feel sick at the sight of a slightly churned up corpse, in fact. The last few months alone had turned up bodies devoured by crabs, bears, and with parts cut off by serial killers. The Birdman's body was tame in comparison.

"You can take a break if you need to," Sadie murmured quietly to O'Hara, out of earshot of the others. O'Hara shook his head in a fierce movement.

"I'm fine," he insisted, and Sadie smiled approvingly to herself. There would have been no shame in the rookie accepting her offer, but she found herself glad that he hadn't. He was determined to prove himself, much as she had been in her early days. She would be giving a good report of O'Hara back to Golightly.

"As you thought, I would say this was a straightforward crash," the doctor said. He sounded sad, and Sadie suspected that, as a local, he would have been fond of the Birdman too. The sheriff had stepped outside once he had identified the body, not wanting to watch the processing of his friend's corpse. "He was likely dead upon impact."

"Driving too fast?" Harding asked. The doctor nodded.

"I would say so, given the obvious force of the impact."

Harding nodded, looking satisfied. The fact that there was no indication of foul play made this a lot less complicated. In fact, it was almost neat. Sadie felt certain that the British senior detective would see this as a perfect opportunity to wrap up the case without any loose ends, and as the woman spoke again, she confirmed Sadie's thoughts.

"It seems fairly clear what happened here then, I would say," Harding said brusquely. "Tenby—the Birdman—must have run back to

107

his boat, realized that we had gotten there before him and would have found evidence of his guilt, and was fleeing the area. Driving too fast in his panic. He must have known we would be coming to arrest him as soon as we had found the knot and examined his GPS tracker. Of course, he would want a head start on us. Unfortunately, these roads aren't safe at any speeds, I would imagine. And so he went off the road. It's a shame," she mused, sounding almost as though she was talking to herself, "because we will never know the precise details of his plans with Summers, but at least we can be assured that there will be no more killings."

Sadie shook her head, exasperated that Harding, who was clearly no slouch, was happy to wrap things up like this for the sake of a quick flight home. "But this is all conjecture," she argued. "It's guesswork. Informed guesswork, maybe, but still just guesswork. We can't know for certain that we are right about what has been happening here."

Harding turned cool gray eyes on her, and in spite of the other woman's composure, Sadie could sense that Harding was annoyed at her.

"I appreciate your need to play devil's advocate here, Agent Price," the British woman said, resuming her condescending tone of earlier, as though their touching moment outside the tavern had never happened. "But I'm not sure what you are suggesting we do. Question a dead man?"

"Question the locals at the tavern again," Sadie argued. "Question the derrick hands on all three rigs again, this time about the Birdman. I'm not doubting that he was involved, but I don't buy the idea that this was all down to him, or even him and Summers. Are we seriously suggesting that he killed Ed Summers? Summers could have overpowered him in a heartbeat."

"As I said," Harding said slowly, "we may never know all of the details, but how can we know? Both Summers and Tenby are dead. There are no other suspects. You can reexamine everyone if you wish, Agent Price, but we are here to investigate the death on our rig, and I'm satisfied that we have enough answers to close the case." She looked at her colleague over the Birdman's corpse. "Detective Inspector Sheehan? What are your thoughts?"

Sheehan gave his characteristic shrug, and Sadie knew even before he spoke that he was going to agree with his partner.

"I'm sorry, Agent Price," he said gruffly, "but I think this is a pretty clear-cut case You're overthinking and overcomplicating matters. And there are no more leads to chase. Going over and over things is a waste of time and police resources. We're out of this. What you do isn't under our jurisdiction, but I'm not willing to go over ground that we have already covered here when the only people that could fill in any missing gaps in our knowledge are lying dead."

Sadie looked at Agent O'Hara, needing his support to try and convince the Brits not to abandon the investigation, but he shifted from one foot to the other, looking uncomfortable. He didn't meet her eyes as he replied, and she already knew what he was going to say.

"I don't know," he said. "I feel frustrated too, but I think Detectives Harding and Sheehan are right. I don't see what else we can learn by covering old ground."

Sadie glared at him, even as she knew she was being unfair. He was offering his honest opinion and she thought more of him for giving it than simply agreeing with her to try and curry favor, but she was also disappointed that he couldn't see what she was seeing.

"Think about it," she argued. "We only have circumstantial evidence here. That wouldn't be enough for a court of law. We're convicting Tenby and Summers on the basis that they are not here to offer any kind of defense. Even if we accept they were definitely involved—which I agree must be the case—how do we know there weren't others? That there isn't still a mastermind out there, who may not give up? Because if we're wrong," she insisted, "then the consequences could be more dead bodies. What we know of Tenby so far doesn't strike me as a strategic mastermind," she went on. "How did he manage to get aboard three different rigs in less than three days and execute three different men—four if we potentially include Ed Summers? He has no record to suggest he's capable of any of this. Nothing. Nada. He's a wildlife rescuer, not a killer or even an ecoterrorist like Summers."

"Summers did the killings," Sheehan argued.

"The knots were found on the Birdman's boat," Sadie argued.

"Exactly," Harding sniffed. "All the evidence was on his boat. His. Tenby's, or the Birdman's, whatever we want to call him. I'm not sure what more we need, Agent. And presumably he and Summers used the same vehicle for most of the operations. Summers only took his dinghy that final time because we had held him up."

"And he just happened to make it to the Arctic Treader just in time to help the Birdman kill Joliffe and string him up?" Sadie argued back, fighting to keep a tight rein on her flaring anger. She couldn't believe that Harding was refusing to see her point.

Harding shook her head almost pityingly, which only infuriated Sadie even more. "Sometimes, Agent Price," she said sagely, "if you keep scratching at something, you don't uncover anything new. You just end up with an ever-oozing mess. As far as we're concerned, this case is over. I'm going to arrange the helicopter to take us to civilization immediately so that we can get an early flight back to the UK tomorrow."

Sadie saw the relief on Sheehan's face and knew that there was no point in arguing with the British detectives. As far as they were concerned, the case was over. Even O'Hara, her own partner on this, agreed with them. Sadie was just making herself look deliberately antagonistic by continuing to argue.

"Okay," she said at last, sighing heavily. "You're right. Sometimes we just have to accept that there may always be unanswered questions. It was great working with you. I hope you have a safe flight back."

She turned and walked out of the room without waiting to hear their goodbyes. She heard O'Hara hurrying after her, but she quickened her pace, not wanting to talk to him right now.

It galled her to have to give in.

Especially when all of her senses were screaming at her that she was right.

There was still a killer out there, and they were about to let him walk away completely free.

And that meant he could—and no doubt would—kill again.

CHAPTER TWENTY ONE

Sadie was relieved that she didn't have too far to go. The Prudhoe Bay sheriff had booked them into a local motel so that she and O'Hara didn't have to try and get back to Deadhorse at this time of night, although it looked about as welcoming as the former, with an equally gruff landlady.

After being shown their rooms, Sadie and O'Hara stood awkwardly on the landing. Or at least, O'Hara looked awkward.

Sadie was angry. Why was it, she thought, that she was constantly being told how amazing her professional reputation was, how she was wasted up at the Alaska Field Office, and that she was a local hero, yet every time she had an intuition on a case, or went against the status quo, she had to fight to be heard? Once, she would have put it down to being a female in a man's world, but having met Harding, she wasn't so sure.

Most people, she decided, just wanted a simple answer. Or if not simple—because there was nothing about this case that was straightforward—then at least quick. Then the paperwork could be filed, and everyone could get home to bed, and to hell with the truth.

Deep down, Sadie knew she was being more than a little unfair to her colleagues, but she was simmering enough not to care.

"You could have backed me in there," she said to O'Hara, who looked horrified at her words.

"I'm sorry," he stammered, looking like a naughty schoolboy about to be told off. "I thought you wanted my opinion. An honest one."

His reaction cooled her temper and she eyed him with a begrudging admiration. He could have agreed with her just to curry favor, which, considering how starstruck he always was around her, she had half expected. But he had stuck by what he thought was right. She couldn't reprimand him for that; it was the mark of a good agent.

"I did," Sadie sighed. "I'm sorry. I just think wrapping up this case here is a mistake. We're missing something, and I can't just ignore that."

O'Hara nodded, although he looked confused. "What do you think we're missing?" he asked. "I mean, it does all seem a bit too coincidental. Both suspects just happen to be in tragic accidents. I agree with you there. But how do we investigate when there's no evidence that they weren't accidents?"

Sadie didn't reply, annoyed that he was right, and she knew it. There was no concrete lead to be investigated. Sometimes, fate did intervene, and crazy coincidences did happen.

Except that no matter how much she tried to tell herself that, she just couldn't buy it.

"Let's get some sleep," she said wearily to O'Hara. "Maybe things will look different in the morning. I'm exhausted; you must be too."

O'Hara nodded, looking relieved that he had been let off the hook. "Yeah. Are all your cases like this?"

Sadie couldn't help but laugh, which lightened the atmosphere. "You have no idea," she said wryly. "This one hasn't nearly killed me, for a start. Goodnight, O'Hara."

He smiled at her, looking pleased to be in her good books again, and Sadie let herself into her room. It was, she was relieved to feel, warmer than the Deadhorse motel. Other than that, however, it had little to recommend it. The bed looked hard and narrow and there were no shower facilities, just another small sink and a none too clean looking toilet.

She sat down on the edge of the bed, which proved to be as uncomfortable as she had thought, and rubbed her face in her hands. Her body felt bone tired, but her mind was wired as different possible scenarios raced around in her head.

There was a third person, there had to be. Someone who had been pulling Summers's and the Birdman's strings, assuming that they were even involved.

But they had to have been. No matter what she had tried to tell herself out on the landing, Sadie knew one thing; she didn't believe in fate. One of the deaths could be a fatal accident or a misstep, sure, but not both. Sadie didn't gamble, but she knew ridiculously long odds when she saw them.

She tried to tell herself to forget about it and get some sleep. She could go over it again in the morning before they went home, perhaps with Golightly, and maybe things would make more sense.

But instead of undressing and getting into the bed, Sadie found herself pacing the room, going over everything that had happened and every interview that had been conducted and trying to work out what crucial part of the puzzle they had all missed.

But she could think of nothing. She was getting more and more frustrated with herself when her phone rang, startling her.

Cooper.

"Hey. Any more luck today?" His warm, rich voice came over the phone, bringing with it such a stab of homesickness that Sadie almost wanted to cry. *Get a grip, Price,* she told herself savagely. *It's been two days.*

"I should be coming home tomorrow," she told him. "It looks as though everything is all wrapped up. We got our guy. Who is now conveniently dead. He drove his car off the road when we were on our way to arrest him."

There was a pause while Cooper digested her words. "Okay," he said eventually. "It sounds as though things have sped up. And I can also tell from your tone of voice, having been here too many times with you, that you don't buy whatever the official story is."

Sadie couldn't help but laugh. "Am I that obvious?"

"To me," Cooper said wryly. "I'm usually the one on the other end of arguing with you. But who was the guy? The activist that you locked up last night?"

"No," Sadie said, aware, now that she was saying it all out loud to fresh ears, just how convoluted this case was.

Which convinced her that she was right.

"No? What happened to him?" Cooper sounded bemused.

"He's dead too. We found him at the site of another murder this morning with his neck broken."

"Whoa, this is crazy." Cooper sucked in his breath. "Tell me from the beginning."

Sadie told him, beginning with discovering Ed Summers had broken out of jail, Joliffe's murder, the Birdman's boat and subsequent murder. As Sadie was talking, a memory from that evening jolted her.

"Superintendent Harding didn't check the locker on Tenby's boat," she said excitedly. "Once she had found the coordinates on the GPS, we went straight to the tavern to arrest him, assuming, I suppose, that we could go back once we had his statement. But then he died—or was killed—and she made the decision to wrap it up."

"Okay," Cooper said slowly. "I can see why you don't sound happy with this. I wouldn't be either. There are too many coincidences and too many unanswered questions."

"Exactly," she said, feeling gratified. When Cooper paused, she said, "Now you're going to hit me with a *but*, aren't you?"

"Yes, I am," Cooper confirmed, making Sadie groan. "*But* that's not a reason to go do anything rash or put yourself in any danger."

"It's not as though I deliberately put myself in danger, Cooper," she countered. "Sometimes it just kind of comes with the job, you know?"

"And I thought it was because you liked me rescuing you," Cooper teased. Sadie made a retching sound down the phone, and he laughed. It was a nice sound. It was funny, she reflected, how once upon a time Sheriff Cooper had been a thorn in her side and was now rapidly becoming one of her best friends.

Or maybe more than that?

She quashed the thought quickly.

"Cooper, I need to get a look at that boat," she said. "Just in case. If I don't find anything that gives me a lead to investigate, I'll drop it. But I have to try."

Cooper sighed loudly down the phone, serious again. "Price, you're in the middle of nowhere, you're not on your home turf up there. You can't go rogue. And it's the middle of the night. Wait until the morning and talk to the sheriff; he can go through the locker with you."

"The sheriff wants this done with too," she argued. "He wasn't happy about us searching the boat in the first place."

"Speak to Golightly, see what he can do."

Sadie groaned impatiently. "Golightly just wants me back in Anchorage," she said, "and he will want a quick end to this too. I might be able to convince him, but what if it's too late?"

"If there is anything on that boat, it will still be there in the morning," Cooper said sensibly. "Get some sleep, Price, and look at it with fresh eyes tomorrow."

"Yeah," Sadie said, feeling deflated. "You're right. I'll call you in the morning."

They said goodnight, and Sadie lay back on the bed, still fully clothed, staring at the ceiling. Cooper was right, and she knew he was. Surely, there was nothing that could happen overnight. Even if there was another killer out there, he had to be spooked by how quickly they had closed in on Summers and the Birdman. She could go over the boat again in the morning. And if she didn't find anything, then she could go home.

Twenty minutes later, Sadie was walking determinedly back down the wharf.

114

If there was anything to be found on the Birdman's boat, then she was going to find it.

Tonight.

CHAPTER TWENTY TWO

Sadie climbed aboard Birdman's boat once again, shining her flashlight around to have a closer look. She wanted to get a look at that unsearched locker.

The boat felt abandoned and almost eerie now that she knew its owner was dead, lying in the makeshift morgue at the Prudhoe Bay station, his career as a local activist and hero well and truly over.

Maybe this case really was over, Sadie thought, second-guessing herself now that she was alone in the cold and the dark, feeling as though she was chasing shadows. If she had been so sure that they had gotten the wrong guy, then she would have dragged O'Hara along with her to search the boat, no matter how much he protested, she acknowledged to herself. Even Cooper, who had more reason than most to trust Sadie's instincts, had told her to go to bed.

But then, that's how it always went, she grinned wryly to herself. She ran her thoughts past Cooper, he tried to talk her out of them, and she generally turned out to be right. Sadie would have been more likely to forget the idea and go to her bed if Cooper had encouraged her.

Maybe I do need to learn to take direction a lot better, she thought, an image of the Mangler coming back unbidden. Her tendency to go off as a lone wolf had gotten her in more than a few dangerous situations. Sometimes she wondered how many lives she had left, because she must be catching up on the average cat by now.

She found the locker, prying it open with a crowbar that lay near the ropes. The same ropes where O'Hara had spotted the French bowline. Everything pointed to the Birdman, so much so that if Sadie was giving herself advice, she would be telling herself to stop being so stupid and just look forward to getting home the next day.

But it just didn't make sense to her. Yes, Birdman had the boat, which had been in the right place at the right time, and maybe he had teamed up with Summers, who possibly had the physical strength to carry out the murders. Who had lied about his wet clothes and then ran straight to the next murder site. They both had the same motive— hatred of the oil companies for the environmental devastation they

116

undoubtedly caused. And it was just plausible that Summers had simply fallen and broken his neck, and then the Birdman had driven off the road in a panic.

Maybe.

But Sadie didn't deal in "maybes," and there were far too many of them in this case for comfort.

The locker busted open, revealing some clothes and a pile of paper, from scribbled scraps to what looked like plots and charts. Holding her breath, she pulled them out and shone her flashlight on them, rifling through them. She let her breath out in a slow exhale as she read.

Maps of the Beaufort, detailing the precise location coordinates of each rig, and then lists of crew members and even the times of shifts and changeovers. In short, detailed workings of the rigs, including the three where the murders had been committed.

She was just about to look through the scraps of paper when her phone rang.

It was Cooper.

"You're not in bed, are you?" he said before she could speak.

"No, I'm on the Birdman's boat," she said. The noise Cooper made, she wasn't sure if it was a laugh or a groan of exasperation. Possibly a mixture of both.

She read out the contents of the charts to him, and Cooper whistled. "Well, there you go then. There can be no way that he wasn't guilty."

"Maybe," Sadie sighed. "But I just can't buy the idea that this whole thing was just him and Summers. Summers has a record, but it's for more impulsive, overt operations. The Birdman is an animal rescuer, with nothing like this in his past. Analyzing behavior is what I did for years, Cooper, including some of the sickest killers the US has ever seen. You get a feel for these things. And even if Summers and the Birdman are completely guilty, I don't believe they were acting alone."

Cooper was silent for a moment, which Sadie knew meant he was mulling over her theories and taking them seriously.

"But there's no evidence to indicate anyone else, right?" he said eventually. "So even if that's true, what can you do about it? Both of your suspects are dead. Even if there is someone else—or even a group—out there, you've got no leads. But at least you've stopped them in their tracks. Surely there won't be any more killings now."

Sadie didn't answer. She was staring at the piece of paper—a cocktail napkin such as might have come from a bar—and the three words that were scribbled on it.

"I disagree," she said, her tone urgent now. "Whoever is behind this isn't going to want to stop."

"Maybe they have stopped," Cooper argued. "Maybe Joliffe was the final body. They've made their point, surely?"

"Cooper," she said slowly. "I don't think another murder is the next move. I think they're planning something like massive industrial sabotage."

The words swam up at her, bringing with them a memory from the day before that had seemed important at the time but less so as the case had progressed.

Jack-up legs.

The first rig was the largest. And they were planning to seriously destabilize it. And then the others? The killings really were just warnings.

Why else would a napkin on the Birdman's boat allude to the plans she had found scribbled in a derrick hand's notebook? Plans the rig manager had known nothing about?

Plans, she realized, that were due to take place in just a few hours.

Sadie ran a hand through her hair, trying to make sense of it all. If the first victim had been helping to plan this, then why had he ended up dead?

And just how many people were involved in this?

She ran her theory past Cooper, who sounded puzzled.

"But how many people would be needed to pull that off? Surely, they would need the engineer. Who is now dead?"

"Maybe the plans were changed from sabotage to murder," Sadie said quietly. "There's at least one more person involved here. Perhaps he went off plan." Her thoughts flashed to Mike Miller, and the contempt that he had shown for Summers. Could he be involved somehow? Or had she failed to get the measure of Paul Montford?

The more she thought about it, the more she thought Montford could potentially be involved after all. He had seemed genuinely upset about the loss of Chuck, but perhaps it hadn't been him that had killed Chuck. Could that have been Summers?

Sadie shook her head. All she was doing was giving herself more "maybes" to contend with, and that was the last thing that was likely to help. She needed a clear focus. She had a strong intuition that had always served her well, but the complexities of this case made it difficult for her to figure out what was a gut feeling and what was merely her brain working overtime.

The average psychopathic serial killer, she decided, was easier to figure out than this mess.

"This napkin," she said, more to herself than to Cooper. "It could have come from the local tavern, couldn't it?"

"Wouldn't you find them in any tavern?" Cooper argued. "That's a bit of a stretch, even for you."

Sadie ignored his last remark. "Not really," she countered, "when you think how isolated people are here. Apart from Deadhorse, which doesn't even have its own tavern, there isn't another community around for miles. Sure, it could be from someone's house, but this is more like the sort of thing you would see in a bar. Or a restaurant maybe, but there don't seem to be any of them around here. It's a tiny community, Cooper. It makes where I grew up look positively bustling. And think about it, it makes sense. The Birdman seems to be a regular at the tavern. It's going to be the place all the locals congregate, as well as the out-of-town seasonal workers...and the derrick hands. What better place to plan all this than in plain sight?" Sadie could feel herself getting excited, certain that she was onto something.

"Okay," Cooper said slowly. He sounded worried, which was exactly what she would have expected. Cooper knew her too well by now *not* to be worried. "You're going to open this back up, aren't you?"

"If there's any possibility of sabotage, and I just sit on the hunch and it happens, then I'm culpable, Cooper," she argued. "I would rather be wrong and investigate for nothing, than be correct and have it happen right under my nose, on my watch. There has been enough carnage already."

"I get that," Cooper said, and Sadie knew that he did. That he would do exactly the same if he was in her position. "But don't do anything on your own, okay? Take that young agent with you."

There was a slight inflection on the words "young agent" and Sadie couldn't help smiling to herself in spite of the situation. This wasn't the time to tease Cooper for the jealousy that she knew he was capable of experiencing where she was concerned, but she allowed herself a moment of pleasure at the thought.

If she ever got home to Anchorage, then she really had to address whatever was going on between her and Logan Cooper.

"I'll call him now," she promised. "He can meet me at the tavern."

There was a short silence on the other end, and she wondered what Cooper was thinking.

119

Sadie thought she could guess. Their last few cases, which they had worked together more out of circumstance than out of choice, had been harrowing and had ended up with one or both of them in potential or actual life-threatening situations. Where Sadie was impulsive and tended to act on her—professionally honed—instincts, Sheriff Cooper was more logical. He liked to assess risk, whereas Sadie tended to plunge headlong straight into it. That wasn't always a bad thing—Sadie hadn't gained her reputation for being a brilliant agent by playing it safe—but for a solid local cop like Logan Cooper, Sadie knew that he spent more time than was good for him in worrying about her.

"I want you to keep in touch with me," he said. "At least every hour."

Sadie sighed. Perhaps it had been unfair to fill him in on the details of this case, because she had just worried him, and he was too far away to do anything about it, a fact she knew would drive him mad. "Cooper, I'm investigating a complicated case here," she protested. "And I'll have O'Hara. There's no need for you to worry about me."

"It's a bit late for that, Price," he said gruffly. "The last time you told me that and I listened to you, you nearly got yourself killed. I don't want to have to spend my time rescuing you again."

"I've spent just as much time rescuing you," Sadie reminded him. "This isn't a white knight and damsel in distress scenario, Cooper. I'll be fine. But if it makes you feel better, I will keep in touch, okay?"

When Cooper replied, his voice was soft, almost tender. She hadn't been expecting it and his tone made her blush. She was glad he couldn't see her face.

"You had better. I care about you Sadie, you know that."

Uncharacteristically tongue-tied, Sadie didn't quite know how to respond to that. She wasn't great with emotion, and wasn't used to seeing it from Cooper either, at least until recently.

"I will," she reassured him. "I promise," she added. When he didn't reply, she wondered if she should tell him that she cared about him too.

Maybe, even more than cared about him.

But then he spoke, sounding more like his usual self, and the moment was over.

"I want to hear from you every hour, Sadie," he threatened. "Or I'm coming to get you."

CHAPTER TWENTY THREE

Sadie jammed her cell back into the pocket of her parka, cursing O'Hara, who wasn't answering his phone. The young agent was no doubt exhausted and needed to sleep, but Sadie didn't want to waste any time having to go back to the motel to wake him up.

She was nearly at the tavern and was relieved to see that the lights were still on, although she couldn't hear anything like the level of noise that had been coming from the place earlier. She entered to see just a few late drinkers still propping up the bar, including the heavyset guy with the tattoos who had defended Birdman just a few hours earlier. Both he and the bartender looked at her warily.

"Back again?" the bartender asked, deliberately sounding bored, but he flashed the tattooed guy a look that suggested he thought Sadie's reappearance meant nothing but trouble.

The atmosphere was both wary and suspicious, and although Sadie had never been easily intimidated, she felt consciously out of place here. They didn't trust her. But why should they? They wouldn't have heard about the Birdman yet; in fact, it probably wouldn't become local news until the morning, and Sadie felt bad about not giving them the news. But she knew the Prudhoe Bay locals were even less likely to trust her if she disclosed that the Birdman had run off the road, probably as a result of their investigation, and was posthumously going to be blamed for three murders with, in Sadie's opinion at least, nowhere near enough evidence.

She was still sore that O'Hara hadn't backed her up. He was a good agent, but he had a lot to learn about having some loyalty to his partner.

At the same time, she admired the fact that he had the balls to be honest with her. It was a good trait in a federal agent and convinced her even more that he had a good career ahead of him—but she was still pissed at him. She was his senior agent on this case; he could at least show a little deference. Less than forty-eight hours ago he had been starstruck enough that he could barely speak to her without blushing. Now he was actively disagreeing with her professional opinion.

It stung.

Maybe Cooper hadn't been too wrong about her ego issues after all.

As she reached the bar, Sadie tried her best to look relaxed and friendly. To defuse the situation.

"I'm trying to follow a new angle on the spate of crimes on the local rigs," she said to Eddie and the men drinking. She hesitated, wondering how much to let slip, and decided to give them just enough honesty to hopefully open a conversation. "I don't believe the Birdman was responsible, either. But I need to prove that."

The bartender narrowed his eyes at her, but she saw his shoulders relax slightly. The tattooed guy looked more interested too, leaning closer to hear their conversation.

"I'm not sure what I can do to help," Eddie said. "I just tend the bar. I don't quiz my customers on their private lives."

"Do you get the derrick hands from the rigs in here a lot?"

Eddie nodded. "They don't get a lot of time off, but when they do, they pour into here, yeah. And I meet a lot of them coming and going. Many can't hack it for more than a few months; a few of them settle in Prudhoe, although they're not always too popular with the locals. The rigs cause a lot of trouble, especially with the fishermen. 'Course, it's not their fault, we all gotta earn a living, but you know how some folk can be."

"Mm." Sadie nodded encouragingly, sliding onto a barstool. "Were there any…altercations, then? Between the rig workers and local fishermen, maybe?"

Eddie shook his head. "I don't allow any trouble in here," he said. His eyes flickered toward the man with the tattoos as he said it and Sadie wondered if he had been in a fight at the tavern. "You know that, Grayson," Eddie said, confirming Sadie's thoughts.

The man, Grayson, laughed. "I've been in a couple of punch-ups," he said to Sadie, shrugging apologetically. "Not with any derrick hands though. They're usually no soft touch themselves."

Sadie nodded again, thinking of the likes of Paul Montford and Mike Miller. "Did you ever meet a derrick hand named Chuck?" she asked. "An engineer on one of the rigs. Big guy, blond hair. His colleagues say he was a nice guy, didn't like trouble."

Eddie and Grayson exchanged glances again. They knew Chuck, that was apparent.

"He's been in a few times," Eddie said, his expression guarded. "Like you said, he was a nice guy. What do you want with him?"

So, the reports of the murders hadn't mentioned any names. That was a good thing, at least.

"Did he know the Birdman?" Sadie asked, deliberately ignoring Eddie's question. "Or was Birdman unfriendly with the rig workers? It seems like he would be, given his passion for helping out the wildlife that the oil spills have harmed."

Eddie shook his head and turned away. "You're not putting words in my mouth, lady," he said, and started to clean the bar, not looking up at her. Sadie bristled at the "lady," but decided now wasn't the time to pursue it.

Grayson, however, was watching her curiously. "I did see Chuck and Birdman talking," he offered. "But they were friendly."

Sadie felt the hairs prickle on the back of her neck. This was adding up, although she didn't know yet exactly what to. But Chuck had been making notes about the jack-up legs, and Birdman had a note referencing the same thing in his locker; that must have been what they were discussing.

"Do you have any idea what they were talking about?" she asked Grayson, who shrugged and shook his head. Sadie swallowed her disappointment. It was too much hope that the local was about to reveal that he had overhead secret plans to sabotage the rig. If he had, she knew he wouldn't be sharing them with her.

"Why are you sharing this now?" she asked.

Grayson looked surprised. "You didn't say anything about Chuck before. And hey, if it helps get Birdman out of trouble, I'm happy to help."

"He's obviously a very popular guy," Sadie said, taking care not to keep saying "was." The memory of his shattered body at her feet in the snow swam before her eyes and she pushed it away, not wanting Grayson to sense her discomfiture. Sadie was used to keeping things back from the people she questioned—hell, it was a necessary part of the job—but keeping the fact of a friend's death from someone wasn't a good feeling. Especially if the Birdman was as nice a guy as everyone seemed to think.

But there was another thing that didn't make sense. If both Birdman and Chuck were such nice guys, why were they suddenly planning industrial sabotage—or murder?

And how the hell did Chuck end up dead?

123

There were too many loose ends, and every lead she uncovered just seemed to create new ones rather than tying any of them up. She wished she could be more like Harding and just leave it alone.

But her inherent need for justice, something that had driven her ever since her sister's death, would never allow that to sit right on her conscience. If either Summers or the Birdman was innocent, and there was a killer out there, then she had to bring them in.

Then there was the fact that the sabotage plans could still be going ahead if there was a third—or fourth, if one counted Summers—suspect involved in this.

A vague theory was taking shape, but as yet Sadie didn't have a face or a name to put to her hunch. But what if this had indeed been the work of a group, except some of the group hadn't been happy with the plans for murder? And Chuck ended up somehow being the first victim?

Sadie could almost hear Cooper's voice in her head—also accompanied now by Harding's—telling her that her theory was far-fetched. That she was weaving stories out of random hunches.

The problem was, Sadie knew that her random hunches usually turned out to be right.

"Did you ever see Chuck coming in here with anyone else?" she asked. "Maybe another derrick hand?"

Grayson tipped his head to one side, thinking. "Yeah," he said slowly. "There was one guy he came in with a couple of times, but I don't know his name. Chuck would say hello to you, you know? Offer to buy you a drink. The other guy, he had a mean look to him. I remember thinking he was one to keep an eye on. Eddie here likes to moan about me getting into fights," he said with a grin, jerking his head toward the bartender, "but what he didn't tell you is I was usually getting rid of troublemakers for him. He owes me a few free drinks."

Eddie didn't look over at them, having moved on to counting the tips, but he made an audible scoffing noise that made Grayson smile. Prudhoe Bay and its tavern was obviously a close-knit community, and Sadie felt a pang of homesickness as she thought of the saloon, Caz and Jenny, and the Coopers. For so long, Alaska had been only the place that she had run away from. Now suddenly it was home again.

"This other guy," she asked, mulling over the possibilities in her mind, "can you remember what he looked like?"

124

"Not really," Grayson said apologetically, "but I remember thinking that he looked as though he could be one of those troublemakers, like he said. Dark hair, looked strong, that's all I can remember."

Mike Miller, Sadie thought, or more likely, given his proximity to Chuck and the fact that he worked on the same rig where sabotage seemed to be planned, Paul Montford. Sadie inwardly cursed herself at the thought that she had Montford in her grasp yet had ruled him out so easily.

She looked at the clock above the bar. It was nearly midnight. If the planned sabotage was going ahead, then it would be soon. She had to stop it.

"Thank you," she said to Grayson, sliding off her stool. "That's really helpful."

She walked into the women's restroom to call the Coast Guard, and the Guardsman who answered sounded less than convinced by her warning.

"You want me to radio a rig manager to let him know to be alert that someone is about to blow the legs off his rig, but you can't give me any evidence that this is going to happen?" he said incredulously. "I was told this case was closed."

"Well, I'm reopening it," Sadie said firmly. "Tell Mason to keep a watch on a derrick hand named Paul Montford. We need to get out there."

"I can't help with that," the Coast Guardsman said. "I have to be here. There are fishing boats going in and out. You will have to phone the sheriff."

"Thanks," Sadie said sarcastically. The sheriff was no longer at the station, and she had no faith that the local state trooper who answered was actually going to convey her message any time soon.

O'Hara still wasn't answering his phone either. She left him a voice mail, filling him in on what she had found and now knew. Or thought she knew. Then she walked back out into the bar area, her nerves raw with frustration.

"I need a boat," she said to no one in particular. "I need to get out to one of the rigs, and fast."

The few faces that had turned toward her turned away again. Except for Grayson's.

"I've got my fishing boat," he said slowly. "She's seen better days but she's seaworthy. But you know there's a big blow coming in the morning? It could get dangerous."

125

"I don't need you to wait for me," Sadie assured him. "Just get me there. I'll make sure you get paid well for it tomorrow," she promised him when he still looked hesitant.

That did the trick. Shrugging again, Grayson drank the last of his Bud in one go and motioned toward the door.

"Let's go," he said.

Sadie walked out, her stride urgent. There was no time to lose. Part of her wondered if she was really just being crazy this time, but what choice did she have? She would rather be wrong and look crazy than be right and do nothing while the rig was blown up and more people killed.

Whoever this guy was, she was going to get him.

CHAPTER TWENTY FOUR

In spite of the forecast winds, night on the Beaufort was almost eerie, with the only light coming from the pinpricks of the stars overhead and a sliver of a waning moon. Ice floes bumped up against the side of Grayson's boat, which moved silently through the waters like a ghost ship.

Sadie pulled her fur-lined parka around herself and wished that she had opted for a third layer of thermals underneath her already padded winter uniform. At this time of night, the cold was biting.

Grayson's boat had indeed seen better days. It needed a new paint job, and although it was as he said seaworthy, internally it was in disrepair, with broken seats and a navigation system that took some time to get going. Grayson saw her glancing around and shrugged, looking sad.

"This boat used to be my pride and joy," he said. "I can still remember the day I got her. She needs some work, but I don't have the cash right now. Don't know if I ever will." A dark look crossed his face. "Times are hard on the Beaufort lately."

"What do you catch?" Sadie asked, trying to sound sympathetic even though her mind was on getting to the rig rather than the fisherman's plight. "Cod?"

"Yeah. Arctic or saffron—whatever I can find really. Local fishermen are getting squeezed to death around here. The big fishing fleets down south of here do a lot of damage, but the rigs do even more."

Sadie nodded. She knew times were tough for local fishermen and small fisheries situated near the rigs. The oil spills that regularly occurred obviously affected marine life, but it went much deeper than that. On one hand—and it was certainly the official line—offshore drilling aided fishing communities by boosting their economies with revenues and royalties. And many a fisherman had sold his boat and took a job on the rigs, which usually offered a substantial boost in income.

But as ever with such things, Sadie knew that there was a different story too, and it was clearly one that Grayson had become part of. It wasn't just oil spills that were hurting marine life but also the dispersants used to break them up. And even everyday operations on the rigs led to deposits of toxic chemicals and hydrocarbons. Fish stocks were dwindling, and for a fisherman already in competition with the big commercial fleets, it was becoming harder and harder to make a viable living. The fishing and oil industries had been at war for decades, but whereas the big fleets could hold their own, men like Grayson were indeed being squeezed from both sides.

"It must be tough," Sadie said sympathetically.

Then a thought struck her, with such clarity that she couldn't believe that they had all missed it. They had been so focused on the derrick hands themselves, and on the environmental angle because of Summers and then the Birdman, that any consideration of the grudges local fishermen might hold hadn't been taken into account.

She watched Grayson up ahead of her, navigating the boat, and felt herself freeze inside with more than just the cold. Then she exhaled slowly, watching her breath crystalize in the sub-zero air, and told herself to be calm. Grayson had given her no indication that he was anything but sincere, and she was armed; he wasn't. The Coast Guard and, sooner or later, the Prudhoe Bay sheriff and Agent O'Hara would know where she was. There was no need for her to be fearful.

Still, she kept her hand close to the holster.

The ocean was becoming rougher the further out they got, and Sadie could feel the wind starting to pick up. She turned on her flashlight, scanning the waves, and could just make out the rig in the distance. She swallowed her sigh of relief as Grayson turned an innocent face toward her.

"We're nearly there. You want me to send out a signal to alert them? Are they expecting you?"

"Yes," Sadie lied, hoping that it wasn't a lie and the Coast Guard had indeed gotten a message through. That someone might be watching out for her.

"How long have you been a fisherman?" Sadie asked. She was expecting him to answer all of his life, as she knew was typical for small towns like Prudhoe, but his answer made her hand drift further toward the handle of her gun.

"Ten years, more or less," he said, not taking his eyes from the sea and the rig ahead. "I was a military man before that. Fought in the first

Gulf War," he said proudly, even as Sadie moved into a position on her broken seat that would make it easier for her to spring into a defensive crouch.

The military. Usually, military men were easy to spot, in Sadie's opinion, no matter how long they had been in civilian life, but in spite of the tattoos and strong build, Grayson didn't have that certain bearing that usually marked them out.

But if he had been in the army, then she was betting that he would have certain skills.

Like hand-to-hand combat. And maybe even the means to snap a man's neck.

Even if that man knew martial arts.

Sadie's hand tightened around the handle of her gun.

Grayson, however, seemed completely relaxed, continuing to navigate his boat while talking about his service in the Gulf. His words washed over Sadie, who was no longer taking them in.

"Are we nearly at the rig?" she asked.

"Yup," Grayson said casually. Too casually.

There wasn't much battery left in her flashlight, and Sadie didn't want to waste what was left, but there was something in Grayson's voice that made her every nerve stand on end. She turned the light on and swung it over the now choppy waters, spray hitting her face as she leaned over to see more clearly.

She could barely see the rig now; it was just a speck in the distance.

Grayson was taking her in the wrong direction.

"Where the hell are you going?" she asked.

"It's the wind," he said, sounding unconcerned. "We're going to head straight into it if we go directly towards the rig. I'm going around the other side to avoid the blow hitting us dead on. The forecasts weren't good, and I'm not risking my boat."

"Right," Sadie said, then after a pause, "Thanks."

The battery on her flashlight died. It seemed darker than ever now, A sudden gust of wind blew her scarf from her face and caused her to tip in her seat. As she righted herself, she tightened her hand around the handle of her gun, ready to draw if she needed to. Her instincts were telling her to run, which was impossible, or to shoot, but Grayson was still casually standing half turned away from her, concentrating on the boat.

Maybe she was being hypervigilant.

Or maybe hypervigilant was exactly what she needed to be.

The wind was starting to howl now, and the waves had gone from calm to choppy too quickly, the spray hitting her in the face with some force.

"Hold on," Grayson said to her over his shoulder, raising his voice to be heard above the rising wind. "There are some big waves coming. We might take a few good knocks from the ice floes."

"How long before we reach the rig?" Sadie shouted back, feeling around for a line to grab onto as the boat started to lurch alarmingly. She hoped Grayson wasn't being sentimental about his beloved boat's ability to withstand the ocean at its worst.

"Not too long now," he replied. There was an almost singsong cadence to his tone now, and Sadie suddenly knew, without a shadow of a doubt, that the fisherman was lying. He had no intention of taking her anywhere near the rig.

She got to her feet, drawing her gun, just as a huge wave smashed an ice floe into the side of Grayson's boat, shoving her nearly off her feet.

"Hold on!" Grayson shouted, an undercurrent almost of glee in his voice as the boat lurched again, nearly tipping Sadie over the side. She reached for the line even as her legs went beneath her, and her hand closed around a knot. She held onto it, her weight pulling the line down in front of her, just as Grayson turned toward her, his headlamp illuminating it.

She looked down at the knot even as she struggled to right herself, even as her gun arm reflexively went up to aim at Grayson, and in a split second she saw what it was.

A French bowline.

Then Grayson came at her. Everything seemed to be happening in slow motion. The boat lurched again, tipping her off her feet, just as he swung a harpoon at her head.

She shot the gun, which made him jump back, but she was way off balance and the shot went wide. As she pulled herself to a standing position she took aim again, but again the boat lurched, and Grayson swung with the harpoon.

The length of it smashed into her side, not piercing her but causing her to fall onto the side of the boat, pitching forward toward the sea.

Her gun was flung out of her hand, tossed onto an ice floe, and Sadie howled in pain and frustration, grabbing desperately at the side of the boat as she tried to prevent herself from pitching headfirst into the icy waters.

130

Swaying over her, Grayson was trying to get his balance, ready to take another swing with the harpoon.

For a moment, the world seemed to stop turning as Jessica's face seemed to float in the ice in front of her. The day her sister's body had been found in the frozen lakes of the Lynx Lake Loop back in Anchorage came powerfully and painfully to mind, hitting her with the full weight of its devastating grief.

She was going to die like her sister.

Except out here, her body would never be found.

"No!" Sadie yelled, reality kicking back in. A wave tipped the boat in the opposite direction, and she used its impetus to throw herself back on board and then roll away from Grayson, as he was thrown backwards by the lurching of the boat, the harpoon falling from his hands behind him. Going with the motion of the boat, Sadie staggered halfway to her feet and ran to the other end of the boat, crashing into the nets. She crouched behind them, peering out and trying to locate Grayson by the light of his headlamp, which kept disappearing as he rolled around, struggling to get to his feet as the boat lurched this way and that.

He seemed to be hurt, but not, Sadie thought, hurt enough to stop him. She could see him scrabbling around for the harpoon and her heart sank as she saw him lift it and start to get fully to his feet. She felt around for something, anything, that she could potentially use as a weapon, but could feel nothing but heavy nets.

They weren't going to be a lot of use.

Her heart in her mouth, Sadie watched as Grayson came in her direction, the harpoon raised in one hand. His eyes were darting around, looking for her, but it wouldn't take more than a minute for him to figure out where she was hiding.

Because there was nowhere else to go.

She was alone and unarmed on a treacherous ocean, with a killer.

Who was now just feet away and coming for her.

CHAPTER TWENTY FIVE

Sadie kept herself as low and as small as possible as Grayson came toward her, knowing that the nets wouldn't hide her for long. The boat rolled beneath them and through the darkness she could see him fighting for balance, his headlamp bobbing.

He was nearly on her.

"Come on, Sadie," he said, his voice almost a croon, which made him sound all the more sinister. "You can't hide forever. Where are you gonna go?" He chuckled to himself, and Sadie realized that he was insane. Insane, and armed with a deadly weapon.

She was going to need all of her fighting skills to get out of this one, and no small amount of luck, either.

He was nearly on her now.

Judging more by instinct than by sight, Sadie kicked out with her leg, and it met her target. She hooked her foot around Grayson's ankle and pulled, tripping him over and sending him crashing into the nets, almost on top of her. The harpoon flew out of his hand, landing in the ocean with a splash.

Now they were more evenly matched.

Snarling with rage, Grayson lunged at her, but Sadie evaded him, running toward the other end of the boat.

They faced each other, both braced for attack, but neither of them moving now. Then Grayson began to move carefully toward her. Sadie eyed him. He was taller, broader, and stronger, and if he was to be believed, militarily trained. But she was lighter on her feet. If she could evade him for a while, she might be able to gain an advantage.

Of course, it would help if she was on solid ground rather than a creaky old fishing boat on an increasingly tempestuous ocean.

He was almost halfway to her now. Sadie tried a tactic she had used before to buy time in situations like this and which rarely failed to work. If there was one thing that seemed to be consistent with all types of killers, it was the fact that they loved to brag about their plans. About how clever they were, and all of the heinous crimes that they had managed to get away with.

132

"It wasn't you covering up for Birdman when we questioned you in the tavern, was it?" she yelled to him over the roar of the wind and the waves. "It was him covering up for you."

Under the light of his lamp, she saw him smirk, making his heavily shadowed face look almost demonic.

"He didn't know about the killings until you started poking around," he said. "He thought I was using his boat to do reconnaissance, for the sabotage we had planned."

"The bomb?" Sadie guessed. "The rig is set to blow soon, isn't it?"

"That was the plan," Grayson admitted. "But you bozos ruined it by poking around. Then Birdman pulled out. And once he realized he was going to be in the frame for murder, then he started threatening to turn me in. So I threatened him. Told him to get out of town. He was easy enough to scare." He said it in contempt for the bird rescuer, and Sadie felt a flare of anger.

"But you didn't let him get away," she said, backing off as he continued to slowly approach. He was playing cat and mouse with her, and it made her angry. She was no one's prey.

"No. I couldn't. It was easy enough to run him off the road with that death trap he drove. I thought that would be the end of it. Then you turned up, asking questions. But no matter. No one is going to find your body out here," he said matter-of-factly. "I'll let things die down and carry out the bombing myself. It will be better on my own. Birdman thought it would just be a warning, a little bit of damage," he laughed. "He had no idea what me and Ed were really planning."

"You were going to blow the whole rig," Sadie said. "You would kill everyone on board."

"No sense in not doing things properly, is there?" Grayson said, as though it was a perfectly reasonable proposition. Sadie shook her head as she realized how badly she had miscalculated. The bomb wasn't going off tonight. It was still in Grayson's possession. All she had done was put herself out on the ocean alone with a man who had already murdered five people in less than three days.

"So, Ed knew your plans?"

"It was Ed who approached me," Grayson told her. "He knew I hated the oil companies as much as he did, and he knew I'm no stranger to combat." Grayson flexed his muscles in a way that would have been comical if Sadie hadn't been trapped aboard his boat with him.

"So, why kill him?"

133

"Because he was panicking, once you guys arrested him," Grayson said, sounding angry himself now. "He compromised the whole Joliffe operation, coming out to the rig like that. Started talking about how we had to get away there and then. Make a run for it on the boat. I figured if I made it look like an accident and left him at the scene, I could put him in the frame nicely. But you and your Brit friends still didn't stop poking around, did you?"

Sadie grabbed the side of the boat as a large wave nearly tipped her off her feet. Grayson slid across the deck and Sadie waited for an opportunity to pounce, but he righted himself at the last minute.

"But how did Chuck come into this?" Sadie asked, trying to fit the pieces together. "I know Birdman brought him on board, so I'm guessing he didn't know the full extent of the plans either, but why join in at all? He was a derrick hand. And why did you kill him?"

"We needed Chuck to get information about the rig and the jack-up legs," Grayson told her. "But I always knew he was a weak link. He was already starting to have second thoughts. His motives weren't strong enough. He had some issues with the rig manager about shift patterns and underpayment. I knew he would end up backing out. So me and Ed decided he would be the first body. It was impressive, wasn't it, the way we left him hanging?"

Sadie felt sick. Grayson had taken out every one of his partners in crime without a shred of remorse, never being fully honest with any of them. She suspected his motives were less about the oil companies and more about the sheer thrill of bloodshed. Perhaps the army had made him that way, or perhaps that had been his reason for signing up. She suspected the former.

"They didn't deserve to die," she told him, flatly. "None of them. What have you achieved? Even after you blow up the rig, what? Another one will be built. You will get caught. All that blood on your hands, and for what?"

Grayson sneered contemptuously. "You think I don't have plenty of blood on my hands? I was Delta Force, lady."

"That's defending the country. This is taking innocent lives."

"Innocent," Grayson scoffed. "No one involved in Big Oil is innocent. Chuck was part of the problem, and a two-faced coward too. Of course he deserved to die. And Ed was as happy to kill as I am. He would have done the same to me. As for the others, they were oil industry insiders. Targets. No different from my army days."

"And Birdman?" she countered. "A local hero? What did he do to deserve this?"

"He was weak," Grayson spat. "Afraid to do anything more than scare people. Spent his life just cleaning up half dead birds. Pathetic. What does that achieve? Don't give me that bleeding heart nonsense, that changes nothing in this world. You want to make a statement, you gotta do it properly."

They were circling each other now, Sadie moving around the edges of the boat while Grayson pivoted in the middle of the deck. He would be on her in a second, she knew. She had to get the first punch in and knock him off his guard. Unsettle him. He wouldn't be expecting her to be able to fight him, not really.

Sadie hoped he wasn't right.

"That's why you were going to blow up the whole rig."

Grayson laughed. "Lady, I *am* going to blow up the rig. In fact, I'm going to blow up all of them. And you won't be able to do a damn thing about it, because you will be at the bottom of the Beaufort being eaten by fishes."

Sadie sucked in her breath as she realized the extent of his evil plan. Then she slipped as the boat lurched abruptly, righting herself to see Grayson leap across the boat toward her.

His fist traveling toward her through the air.

Just inches from her face.

CHAPTER TWENTY SIX

"Goddammit, Price," Cooper cursed to himself as Sadie's phone once again made a beeping sound and cut him off. It sounded as though she was out of range, which wasn't too surprising given how far north she was, but this was the fifth time in the last twenty minutes that he had tried to call.

She knew he would be calling. Why didn't she move somewhere that she could get a signal? He had been able to speak to her so far.

He tried to tell himself that she was just busy, perhaps questioning someone, and would get back to him when she could, but his attempts to convince himself weren't proving very successful.

What if she was in danger?

This had happened before, and he had been right. Not that Sadie would ever thank him for reminding her. She wasn't the type of woman, as she so often reminded him, who needed rescuing.

Even when she did.

Knowing that getting to sleep would be impossible until he had satisfied himself that Sadie was safe, Cooper got up from where he had been lying fully clothed on the bed and went downstairs. Jane was sitting at the kitchen table, nursing a coffee.

"You're still up?" he asked her, noticing the deep shadows under her eyes. Jane had recently finished helping on the local child abuse case that Sadie had originally uncovered, and although she hadn't spoken to him about it much, he knew his deputy and younger sister well enough to know that it had seriously gotten to her. But then, how could it not? That particular case had left unseen bruises on all of them. The sort that never faded.

"Yeah," she said with a sigh. "Restless mind. How about you? You were at the station at five a.m. this morning. I thought you would be long asleep."

When Cooper didn't answer but took the seat opposite her and sat down with a heavy sigh, Jane looked at him astutely, tucking her short dark hair behind one ear.

"I know that look, Logan. What's going on with Sadie?"

Cooper grimaced, embarrassed that his sister found him so transparent where Sadie Price was concerned. "She's not answering her phone," he said shortly.

Jane raised an eyebrow, looking amused. "That's all? Logan, it's after midnight. She's probably asleep in some motel, dreaming of coming home to you. The sooner the two of you just admit the way you feel about each other, the better."

Cooper glared at her before explaining. "She's gone off investigating on her own. She promised me she would take that young agent who went with her, but you know what's she's like when she's got a nose for a lead. She won't wait for backup. I made her promise to call me every hour, or I would call her."

"Well, there you go," Jane said triumphantly. "I've rarely met a woman so stubborn as Sadie Price. She's probably ignoring you. You won't win her over by playing knight in shining armor, I thought you would have realized that by now." Jane blew into the steam rising from her coffee, rolling her eyes.

"If you would just listen," Cooper said impatiently. Jane sat up, surprised, her eyes registering the realization that her older brother was seriously worried.

"Okay, go on."

"I obviously won't go into details, it sounds like a sensitive case, but she's been working with Scotland Yard on this. And the case was wrapped up earlier today. Everyone has gone home or to bed. Sadie wasn't happy. She's convinced they've got the wrong guy."

Jane frowned. "Has the suspect confessed?"

"He's dead," Cooper said shortly. Whistling under her breath, Jane drummed her fingertips on the table. "Sadie's been right before," she offered.

"I know. Which is why I'm worried. She's chasing a killer around North Alaska, no doubt by herself, and isn't checking in. However stubborn she might be, she would know I'm waiting to hear from her, and she wouldn't let me just sit here worried. Not after the near brushes with death we've both had in the past."

Jane nodded, her dark gray eyes now clouded with the same concern as her brother's. "You're right," she agreed. "She wouldn't. So, what are you going to do? Is there someone you can alert?"

"She seems to think the local law enforcement is pretty useless," he told her. "So I'm thinking Paul Golightly."

They both contemplated the thought of potentially waking Golightly up in the middle of the night.

"Rather you than me," Jane said, taking a sip of her now cooled drink. "What if you're wrong and she turns out to be perfectly fine?"

"I'd rather that than be right, no matter how pissed Golightly gets at me," Cooper admitted. He cleared his throat. "Do you think he will let me use the FBI helicopter?"

Jane blinked at him. "No," she said shortly. "I think he will tell you to go take a hike, to put it politely. It's worth a try though, I suppose."

"I could at least try and find out if she is actually with the other agent," he said. Jane nodded.

"Good luck," she said. Cooper sighed and walked into the hall to the antique handset, dialing the number he had for Golightly. If he wasn't at the field office, it would go straight through to his cell.

It took three tries before Golightly picked up.

"This had better be good, Sheriff," the older ASAC growled down the phone. "How many bodies?"

"None, yet," Cooper said. "This is about Sadie. I think she might be in trouble."

Golightly groaned audibly. "Brilliant as she is, Agent Price is always in trouble. What has she done now?"

Talking quickly, before the ASAC could interrupt and tell him he was talking nonsense, Cooper gave him a run-down of the situation. Golightly didn't sound impressed.

"She probably doesn't have a signal, Sheriff," he pointed out. "You're suggesting I launch some rescue operation just because she has gone AWOL for less than an hour? This is Price we're talking about."

"But if there's still a killer out there—"

"That's a big *if*, Sheriff. Even Price has to get it wrong sooner or later. Look, I know you two have something going on—"

"There's *nothing* going on," Cooper snapped, feeling horrified at the idea that it was obvious to the whole of Anchorage how he felt about Agent Price. "Could you at least find out if she is with the agent you sent with her?"

"O'Hara? He's wet behind the ears. I was betting Price would give him the slip. Look, Sheriff, this is what she does, and she may not be the most orthodox agent, but she gets results."

"With respect, sir," Cooper said through gritted teeth, "she very nearly died on the last case. Surely her life is not less important than results."

138

There was a silence, and Cooper sensed that the older man was furious at the implication. When he spoke, though, he had taken Cooper's words on board, to the sheriff's surprise.

"Fair enough, Sheriff. Give me ten minutes to get these old bones out of bed and I'll call you back."

Cooper paced the hall while he waited, while Jane stood in the doorway of the kitchen, watching him. When the phone rang, Cooper snatched it up.

"Golightly?"

"It's me. She's not with Agent O'Hara. It took me five attempts to wake the lazy bones up. He doesn't know what you're talking about. He went back to the motel with Price and went to bed. He said she was annoyed no one listened to her about there being another suspect, but she agreed to leave it until the morning. Which obviously she didn't, as you know. So O'Hara knows less than you do. He did say she had attempted to call him though, but he slept through."

So she did listen to me, Cooper thought, trying not to want to wring the young agent's neck for sleeping through the call. It was the first time O'Hara had worked with Sadie, how could he know that there was no way she would have just gone to bed if she was convinced they had the wrong guy?

He had to get up there, he thought, trying not to panic. When he suggested the helicopter, however, Golightly cursed at him down the phone.

"On a hunch? It's not even a local sheriff matter."

"The local police department will foot the bill for the fuel and pilot," Cooper told him, avoiding Jane's eyes. The Anchorage station was in the red at the best of times. "I'm certain Price is in danger, sir. She knows I'm waiting to hear from her. She would have attempted to get in touch."

"You're probably wrong. It's a wild goose chase," Golightly argued.

"And what if I'm not?" Cooper argued.

Golightly let out a low, drawn-out groan, and Cooper knew he had him. Golightly would never let him forget it if he was wrong. But he also knew that for all the ASAC's reticence, he cared about his agents and held Sadie in high regard. He wouldn't play Russian Roulette with her life.

139

"All right," Golightly snapped eventually. "It will be ready within the hour. And you will be paying for it." He put down the phone before Cooper could respond.

Cooper grabbed his coat.

He was going to find Sadie.

Before it was too late.

CHAPTER TWENTY SEVEN

Grayson was strong and he put his whole weight behind his punch, but Sadie was ready for him, instantaneously bracing herself and lifting her hands into guard without even having to think about it. Quantico had taught her well.

As a result, the fisherman's fist just grazed her cheekbone, but even that sent her spinning backwards, perilously close once again to the side of the boat. Had he hit her full force, she knew he would have easily broken her nose, if not completely knocked her out cold.

She had to stay on her feet and make sure that didn't happen.

As he came for her again, she pivoted quickly, kicking out sideways and planting her leather boot firmly in his groin. He howled in frustration, and she would have allowed herself a smile of satisfaction if the boat hadn't lurched again and tipped her off balance.

Luckily, Grayson was still clutching at his testicles, and she was able to half run, half crawl, further up the boat away from him, searching frantically with her hands for the weapon. As she did so she realized there was a little more light that wasn't coming from the fisherman's headlamp, and she looked up and over the waters.

They were approaching a rig. The boat had been left to itself while Grayson had been playing cat and mouse with her around it, and the wind had blown it according to its own whims. She couldn't be certain it was the same rig she had been originally aiming for, but it didn't matter.

An oil rig meant people. And that meant help.

Assuming, of course, that anyone was awake and happened to be looking down in their direction. Even so, it was better than being stranded without a soul around with the madman who was currently getting to his feet and charging toward her in the gloom. Sadie looked around her briefly. There was nowhere to go.

She started to back away in a defensive position, heading backwards toward the controls where she hoped she could manage to set off an alarm signal that could be heard as they drifted toward the rig.

141

She had to be careful, though. If Grayson realized what she was doing he could take control of the boat again and send them veering off in the opposite direction.

Sadie's quick mind weighed him up as he came toward her. She had taken down bigger men than Grayson without fear or even much thought, but he was a tougher adversary. It wasn't his strength so much as the prowess from what he claimed was military training. He had snapped Ed Summers's neck with his bare hands. That wasn't something Sadie could do.

For the first time since becoming a federal agent, she felt outmatched in a fair fight. She needed to keep space between them, but that was going to be far from easy on the boat.

She danced back as he came toward her, still thinking about that alarm signal, when her foot hit something unseen on the floor and she stumbled back and off to the side, well away from the controls and toward the edge of the boat. In a second, Grayson was pouncing on her, pushing her down to the bottom of the boat with his hands aiming for her throat.

A wave came crashing over the side, knocking him sideways. Seeing her chance, even as the salt water crashed over her, Sadie's hand flew upwards, hitting Grayson's nose with the heel of her palm. She heard the crunch of bone breaking and a popping sound and his feral howl of pain. His hands left her throat and she scrambled to her feet, dashing for the center of the boat, away from the waves that were now crashing over the sides, trying desperately to balance in the tilting, lurching vessel.

Grayson came at her with a roar, and although she hopped swiftly to the side the unstable flooring was against her and he tripped her with his foot as she wobbled unsteadily. In a second, he was on top of her, wild fury in his eyes and blood pouring from his nostrils as he rained blows down on her. She tried to defend herself, but one of her arms was trapped under his knee and she couldn't stop a lot of his blows from landing fully. Her face was going to be beaten to a pulp after this.

If there was an "after this." She had no doubt that Grayson would kill her and throw her body in the Beaufort. Summoning every ounce of her strength and focus, she jabbed at his eyes with precision, gouging at them with two fingers. He howled again, and his weight eased off her enough that she was able to roll to the side and jump to her feet. He followed her, but unsteady and with only half his vision, Sadie punched him squarely in the jaw. It sent him reeling backwards, but she knew it wasn't enough to knock him out. If anything, she was just making him angrier and more determined to kill her.

The rig was looming overhead now, and the waves were tossing the boat around on top of the sea like a dog with a plaything. They were being thrown perilously close to the stanchion.

Not giving Grayson time to recoup, Sadie went on the offensive, following her first punch with two more, each well landed. But Grayson could fight, and he got her with a right hook to the side of her head that sent her spinning off toward the net. He grabbed her by the shoulder and punched her hard in the stomach.

It was enough to knock the wind out of her, and she bent over instinctively, struggling for breath. But she was still alert, clocking his every move, and as his foot came toward her face Sadie grabbed his ankle and twisted hard, sending him crashing down to the deck.

"Bitch," she heard him grunt as she backed away, preparing herself for his next onslaught. She knew she couldn't beat him by wrestling down on the ground, he was too strong. Her only hope was that he would tire out faster than her, or that she managed to tip him over the side.

A sudden, huge wave tipped up the entire front of the boat, lifting her off her feet and sliding her down the boat, past Grayson, who was hurtled into the side of the boat. She hit the deck with force, and the water crashed down on her, leaving her choking and momentarily unable to move under its weight. As it passed, she could hear Grayson spluttering too, not far from her, and scrambling to get to his feet.

Shaking the water from her eyes, Sadie rolled away from him, clutching at the side of the boat as it tipped again, knocking Grayson flat.

It was looking highly likely that the ocean was going to kill them both. Holding onto the side, she started to haul herself around the edge of the boat, trying to make it back to the heavy nets, which might at least provide some cover from the waves. Another wave crashed overboard, just missing Sadie but smashing squarely into Grayson.

Her muscles screamed as she dragged herself toward the nets, and her face was as covered in blood as Grayson's. She looked around and saw with a shock that they were nearly under the rig itself. She thought again about sounding the alarm, but that would have meant both moving in Grayson's direction and putting herself more at risk of being washed overboard. Her head ached as she tried to think through her next move.

Sadie could climb, but so could Grayson, and likely better than her, considering that he had been doing a lot of it lately with his getting up on the rigs and then climbing the towers. Trying to outclimb him up the stanchions would be madness.

But it might be her best option to stay alive, she thought. He was hurt too, and although he was stronger, she was smaller, lighter, and quicker. It might give her an advantage.

She hauled herself up to a crouch, watching the approaching rig and trying to judge her escape. The way the boat was being tossed around and the force of the waves, if she timed this wrong, she could be crushed against the stanchion rather than having any chance of climbing it.

Then, in the gloom, she saw the size of the wave that was rushing toward them, and as she felt it lift the boat up into the air, she flattened herself against the side and hung on for dear life, bracing herself for the approaching impact against the steel of the rig.

Time seemed to slow down as the boat tipped, her side going briefly under. Icy water filled her eyes, ears, and nose and, even as she clamped her mouth shut, her lungs. There was a fierce roaring in her ears, and she could feel the pull of the undercurrent, threatening to drag her down.

So far down that she may never come up again. Not alive, at any rate.

She clutched on to the side with every last bit of strength that she possessed, feeling her lungs burning as she fought not to inhale. She needed air desperately.

Where was Grayson?

Finally, she felt the boat rising again and bursting through the surface, leaving her coughing and struggling to catch her breath. Her vision started to clear just as she heard a loud crack and saw the heavy timber falling toward her as the boat started to split. Letting go of the side she rolled, her hands up over her head to protect herself. But the wood landed on her legs, making her scream out loud, although thankfully she avoided the full impact.

Where was Grayson?

As the boat landed fully back into the water, he landed heavily on what was left of the upper deck, and as Sadie stared at the sight before her, she realized what had happened. The boat had been thrown against the stanchion, splitting it, and Grayson had gone with it. As he thumped down onto the deck, Sadie could see the force of the impact had

144

crushed his face and torso to a bloody mess, bone showing through the skin. She looked away, momentarily sickened, then as she looked back, she watched his body slowly roll into the sea, through the broken side of the boat.

Two things became clear to her at once.

Grayson was dead and could no longer try to hurt her.

But the boat was going to sink, and she was currently trapped, with not enough energy to get herself free. Even if she could get herself from under the timber and up onto the stanchion, she wouldn't have the strength to climb. She wasn't even sure if her legs were broken or not. Cold was starting to overtake her body, and she couldn't differentiate between the pain that seemed to fill every inch of her and the icy chill that went to her bones. She couldn't distinguish one body part from another.

Sadie tried to drag her torso across the boat and from under the wood, back toward the controls, but she couldn't move from under the weight, or even manage to properly coordinate her upper body. She gave up, lying back down, a wave of defeat washing over her.

At least Grayson was dead. He couldn't hurt anyone else. All she had to do was hang on. Someone would find her, she told herself, trying to fight against the rising despair that told her that she was going to die here, alone. That by the time anyone found her body she would be frozen stiff.

Like Jessica.

The memory of her sister's corpse swam up in her memory with such clarity that Sadie could almost see her in front of her eyes.

Then the image faded.

It wasn't Jessica's face that was the last one she saw before blackness swallowed her.

It was Cooper's.

CHAPTER TWENTY EIGHT

"Sadie? Wake up, you can't fall asleep."

Sadie blinked up at Jessica, who was smoothing Sadie's damp hair back off her face, her beautiful blue eyes wide with fear.

"My head hurts," Sadie moaned. It was her own fault, she should have known not to challenge their father the way she had, not when he was that drunk and in a mood like a bear with a sore head. But Sadie never could keep her mouth shut. Unlike Jessica, who was quiet and pleasant and whom everyone loved, Sadie had a mouth on her and an attitude to match.

It was no wonder that Jessica was their father's favorite. Not that it meant much, other than it was Sadie who felt his fist rather than her older sister. He still didn't come home from the saloon, or buy food for the cabin, or logs for the fire. Ever since their mother's death from cancer Jessica had played mom to her little sister.

Sadie adored her.

"I just want to go to sleep, Jessie," she moaned, raising a hand to her head. He had hit her so hard this time that she had fallen and smashed her head on the grate. Then he had stormed out, ignoring Jessica's screams.

"Miss Tyler at school says you shouldn't sleep straight after a bang on the head," Jessica insisted. "You might never wake up again."

"That's only if you vomit. And Miss Tyler smells," Sadie retorted. "Honestly, Jessie, I'm fine."

Her sister wrapped herself around her on the narrow bed, pulling their one thin blanket over them both. Sadie let herself drift, soothed in the warmth of her sister's skinny arms.

She wanted to drift off and never wake up.

Sadie, wake up....

...wake up, Sadie.

Her eyes snapped open, the smell of salt hitting her, the sound of her sister's voice still lingering on the air.

"Jessie?" Sadie croaked, full of sudden longing as she looked around to see where the voice was coming from.

But Jessica wasn't here.

Sadie was still on the boat, or what was left of it, wedged between the stanchions at the bottom of the rig. She was so cold she could barely feel her body, although there was enough of a dull ache for her to know that if she ever got out of here, she was going to feel it for days.

If she ever got out of here... Water was lapping perilously close. The boat was slowly sinking, and her legs were still trapped. If hypothermia didn't get her, then she would drown.

But there was no time to panic. She heard a shout, and then blinked as she saw the dinghy being lowered down from the rig just feet away from her. Near the flow where Grayson's body still lay, no doubt frozen rigid by now.

"Help...over here..." Sadie croaked weakly. It was enough. A spotlight hit her full in the face.

"There's another one over here! I think she's alive!" came a voice that Sadie vaguely recognized.

She had been found.

Her energy spent, she blacked out again.

*

Drifting in and out of sleep, Sadie once again heard a familiar voice dragging her back to consciousness. But it wasn't Jessica's this time.

Cooper?

She was sure she could hear his voice as she swam groggily back to consciousness, and she told herself that she had to be delirious.

Or dead.

Where was she?

For a start, the biting, icy cold had gone, and although her clothes were damp next to her skin, she felt as though she was swathed in blankets on top of them. She was inside, lying down, on a bed. Or, more accurately, a bunk.

She remembered Grayson coming toward her in the gloom, harpoon in hand, and her eyes flew open in a panic.

"Sadie, it's okay. You're safe. You're on board the rig."

The room spun in front of her, and she felt pain slice her body as she reoriented herself to reality. As her vision settled, she saw two figures standing over her, one close, one on the other side of the room.

147

Mr. Mason looked at her from over by the door, and standing over her, concern and worry etched all over his handsome face, was Sheriff Cooper.

Sadie blinked, trying to work out what was happening, but her brain seemed to have turned to cotton wool and her memories were scattered, skittering disjointedly through her mind.

She remembered Grayson coming for her, and then the two of them fighting as the ocean roiled around them. Her face and body throbbed, and she remembered the force of his blows, and then the waves sending them both crashing onto the deck.

She couldn't seem to remember why she had been on his boat on the first place. Her head throbbed with pain, and she tried to pull a hand out from under the blankets to rub her temple, but she was so weak she could only raise it an inch before it flopped back onto the bed by her side.

"Sadie, don't try and move. You need to rest."

It was Cooper's voice again. Her eyes settled on his face, and his familiar features felt comforting to her, even as she wondered again if she was imagining things. He should be back in Anchorage, not here on the Beaufort.

"What are you doing here?" she croaked, her tongue thick and dry in her throat. Copper sat on the side of the bed next to her and chuckled.

"You never updated me. You said you were going to call every hour, remember? Every time I tried to call, I couldn't get through, like there was no signal. I figured you were either in trouble or had headed out onto the ocean. Turns out I was right on both counts."

Sadie frowned, still struggling to piece her memories of the night together.

Then she realized there was weak sunlight coming through the door. She was in a small room on the upper deck, probably Mason's quarters. She blinked at Cooper.

"Grayson..." she said, willing her brain to work.

"He's dead. We found his body on a nearby ice floe. I'm guessing that he was killed when the boat smashed into the rig. Either that or you're an even better fighter than I thought."

He grinned at her, and she tried to grin back, but she couldn't seem to get her facial muscles to work.

"Who? I thought I recognized a voice..." She trailed off. Talking was a lot of effort right now.

"Some guy called Montford spotted you. Apparently, you had suspected him originally. I don't know how that works, but he seems to have a lot of respect for you. Him and another derrick hand spotted Grayson's body and came to investigate. Just as well they did. The medic said less than another hour and hypothermia would have gotten you."

"When did you get here?"

"This morning. About an hour after they pulled you up." He said it lightly, but she could hear the self-reprimand in his voice that he would have been too late to save her had the derrick hands not spotted the fisherman's body. Sadie knew Cooper would never have forgiven himself.

But at least she hadn't given him the satisfaction of being able to turn up and rescue her, she thought with a smile that hurt her mouth.

"How long have I been out?" She couldn't judge the amount of time that had passed, but Cooper had alluded to the morning, which meant she had been here at least half a day.

"It's nearly eight p.m.," he told her. "So all day, pretty much. You were delirious for a while. In fact," he grinned, unable to stop himself from showing all his even, white teeth, "you told me you loved me."

Sadie glared at him. "I did not!"

"You did," Cooper said, still with that ridiculous grin, and Sadie realized he was telling the truth. She cringed inwardly as the heat of embarrassment flooded her body. He was never going to let her forget this.

"I must have been dreaming," she said.

"About me?"

"Definitely *not* about you."

Mason gave a discreet cough in the background. "I'll leave you two to it," he said. "Whenever Agent Price feels able, your pilot said to tell you the helicopter is ready to take you both home. You're welcome to wait until the morning. This is my bunk, but I'm on a night shift. The Prudhoe Bay sheriff can deal with the body and any paperwork this end. Thank you for catching him, Agent Price. We all wanted justice for Chuck."

Sadie watched him go and then turned her attention back to Cooper, who mercifully had stopped grinning and, momentarily at least, had forgotten Sadie's apparent confession of love for him while semi-conscious.

"How did you even get here?"

149

"I convinced Golightly to let me use the chopper. I knew there was something wrong when I couldn't get through. That intuition of yours is rubbing off on me."

"Thank you, Cooper," Sadie said in a serious tone. Now it was his turn to look slightly embarrassed as he cleared his throat and looked down at his hands.

"I didn't do anything," he admitted.

"But you tried. You came. That means a lot," she said, her voice soft. Cooper looked surprised.

"I thought you would chew me out for trying to play the hero again."

"Maybe when I'm feeling better." Sadie smiled. She looked at him, at the familiar lines of his face, and had an uncharacteristic urge to throw herself into his arms. Thank God she was too weak and injured to follow through on it.

But it did mean a lot. They had started their first case together almost hostile to each other and at the very least distrusting, and now somehow, she couldn't—and didn't want to—imagine life without him. She swore that she was never going to admit it to him, but she suspected, deep down, that the words she had said while delirious were perhaps not too far from the truth.

That she loved him.

And she had no idea what she was supposed to do about it.

Sadie had had relationships over the years, a few serious, or at least as serious as her career would allow, but she had always been careful to keep her heart very carefully guarded. Life had taught her that the people she loved the most—her mother, her sister—had been cruelly ripped away. The thought of ever getting married and having children and then having something like that happen had kept her resolutely single and any dating partners at arm's length.

She had never wanted to make the same mistake that her mother did either, of giving everything to a man who turned out to be a drunken, violent monster.

Her work had been her first love. The thing that got her up in the morning, that made her feel alive and gave her a passion and a purpose. Men were way down her list of priorities.

Now Sheriff Cooper, in just a few short months, had come along and was threatening to upturn all that, making her feel vulnerable, and in more danger than she had ever felt at the hands of any criminal or on any case.

Because this involved her heart.

"You look miles away," Cooper said. "Are you okay?"

"Sure," Sadie lied. "I was just thinking about everything…the case. I'm glad it's over."

"Me too," he said, smiling, oblivious to her inner conflict.

The case was over.

But something else, Sadie thought, may only be just beginning.

CHAPTER TWENTY NINE

Sadie winced as she stepped down from the helicopter. Her ribs were throbbing, and her legs were still bruised as hell, making her limp as she started to walk across the tarmac.

To her surprise, Golightly was there, waiting for them.

"Price," he said, shaking his head, "what have you done to yourself this time?" In spite of his gruff tone there was genuine concern in his eyes and Sadie felt suddenly overwhelmed with emotion.

"You know me, sir," she joked to cover up the sudden urge to cry, "I like to throw all of myself into a case."

Sheriff Cooper and Agent O'Hara came up behind her, and she saw Golightly give Cooper an approving nod. "You two seem to be becoming quite the pair," Golightly said. Cooper chuckled and then, seeing Sadie's scowl, chuckled again.

"I turned up too late to be of any assistance," Cooper admitted. "Although my hunch was right."

O'Hara coughed, looking embarrassed. "I should have listened to you, Agent Price," he said, not meeting her eyes. "You could have been seriously hurt."

O'Hara had been quiet on the flight home, and although Sadie had assumed he was suffering from airsickness again, she now realized he was beating himself up for not having been with her to confront Grayson.

"You did good, Agent," she told him firmly. "I was impressed with your performance and will be putting that in my report. It was my decision to go straight out to the rig with Grayson. Had you been there, he probably wouldn't have offered to take us, and he would never have been caught. I took a risk and it paid off." She glanced at Golightly, wondering when—because she knew it was going to be a when, not an if—he would reprimand her for that risk-taking. Right now, though, he was nodding at O'Hara.

"I'll want a report from you, too," he said. "Given the international nature of this, it's best we cover our backs."

"Have you heard from Scotland Yard?" Sadie asked. She wondered how Harding would have felt when she heard the news about Grayson.

"Yes. I reported to them as soon as I got the call. Superintendent Harding will call you herself at some point, but she asked me to apologize to you and commend you on your bravery and insight."

"Wow," Sadie said, taken aback. Harding had surprised her again.

"Take a few days off, Price," Golightly told her. "Get some rest. You look like you need it, and I want my best agent in good shape. I'll be sending a glowing report to Quantico. Who knows, it may help your tribunal."

Sadie swallowed a lump in her throat. Unable to answer without betraying her feelings, she simply nodded.

"Your face looks terrible, by the way," Golightly added before walking off. O'Hara shook his head at his superior's departing back and then turned to Sadie, looking embarrassed again.

"Er, it was great to work with you, Agent Price, I learned a lot."

Sadie gave him a smile of genuine warmth. "I'm sure it will be the first of many cases, O'Hara," she assured him. "And it was great working with you too. Please don't beat yourself up about what happened. I took risks. I'm not always great at working in a duo; it's something I need to get better at."

Cooper coughed. "I can attest to that," he murmured. Sadie glared at him, and he shrugged, splaying his hands out with a mock innocent expression.

"They were your words, Price, not mine." He grinned. "I'm surprised Agent O'Hara got back in one piece himself. The first case I worked with you I ended up in the hospital."

"That's because you're a terrible driver," Sadie snapped, although she could feel a smile tugging at the corners of her mouth. Agent O'Hara looked from her to Cooper and back again.

"Er, I'll catch up with Golightly and go back to the field office," he said. "See you soon, Sadie."

He jogged off, and Sadie watched him go, feeling awkward now that she was on her own again with Sheriff Cooper. She was waiting for him to start teasing her about everything she had said while half delirious on the rig.

To her relief, he didn't mention it. "I'll drive you back to the saloon," he said again. "I'm sure Caz and Jenny can't wait to see you."

153

Sadie limped next to him over to his snowcat, noticing him watching her with concern. Thankfully, he knew better than to offer her an arm to lean on. It was just a few bruises.

She knew how lucky she was that nothing had been broken. Taking a few knocks on a case—even brushes with death—was becoming par for the course for Sadie, but this one had shaken her up. Perhaps it was a combination of having been so far from home and the similarities to her sister's death, but she was definitely feeling a lot more fragile than she was used to.

She tried to convince herself that she just needed a good night's sleep. She couldn't afford to be fragile. Her job—and her sheer stubbornness—didn't allow for it.

She climbed into the snowcat, gasping as her thighs and ribs screamed at her for the exertion.

"You could ask for help, Price," Cooper pointed out. "I know you're tough. You don't need to keep on proving it."

"I don't want to fuel your already inflated hero complex," Sadie said sweetly, settling into her seat. Cooper laughed, shaking his head.

"You don't give an inch, do you, Price?"

"You like me this way," she quipped. "Admit it. You like the challenge."

Even as she said it, Sadie realized all the connotations that her words could have and as she met Cooper's eyes a flash of something, a knowledge neither of them was quite ready to admit to, passed between them. Cooper's eyes softened as he gazed at her.

"I'm glad you're okay, Price. I was really worried about you there for a while. I know you probably think I'm crazy, flying all the way out to the Beaufort, but I had a real sense that you were in danger. And you've taught me to listen to instincts like that."

Sadie swallowed hard, feeling a heat rise up in her that had nothing to do with the snowcat's interior heating system.

"Thanks," she said. It wasn't an adequate response, but what else could she say? She had said enough back at the rig, she reminded herself.

And yet at the same time, she hadn't said enough.

*

Sadie watched the fireflies dancing around Caz's wood burner, like scattered embers in the air. Jenny was snuggled up under her shoulder,

154

uncharacteristically quiet, no doubt because it was well past her usual bedtime, and she was hoping Caz wouldn't notice.

Caz came out from the kitchen and handed Sadie a cup of hot cocoa, which Sadie gulped at gratefully.

"Logan just called. He's on his way over," Caz told her, sitting down next to them.

"Cooper? Why?" Sadie stared into her cocoa so Caz wouldn't see her blush. In the past few days, since she had returned from Prudhoe Bay, Sadie hadn't seen or heard from the sheriff. She wasn't sure if she was disappointed or relieved about that, but she had spent most of the past few days thinking about him.

Caz grinned. "Maybe I just wanted a look at that pretty face of his."

Caz had a longstanding crush on the sheriff that was news to precisely no one, and a source of great embarrassment to him. Underneath that, though, Caz and Cooper were firm friends. Caz also rarely resisted a chance to play cupid between him and Sadie.

"Don't give me that. You're trying to set us up again, aren't you?" Sadie accused.

"Nope." Caz shook her head. "He called me, remember. He said he needed to talk to you. I'm guessing about your father's map?"

Caz was the only other person who knew that Sadie and Cooper were investigating the cold case of Jessica Price's death. She knew both what it meant to Sadie and how difficult the whole subject was for her.

Sadie nodded. They weren't going to go into any details about that in front of Jenny. "Okay."

She heard boots approaching and looked up to see the sheriff, right on cue, coming round the back of the saloon into Caz's yard.

"Hey, Logan." Caz grinned appreciatively, before holding her hand out to a sulkily pouting Jenny. "Come on, little lady, time for bed. Give Sadie a hug."

Sadie squeezed the little girl tight, watching her with affection as they left. Caz discreetly shut the porch door behind them, leaving Sadie and Cooper alone in the yard.

"How are you feeling?" Cooper asked, squatting down next to her and examining the bruises on her face. The swelling was going down, but her skin had erupted in a kaleidoscope of yellows, browns, and grays.

"Everything aches, but I'm not limping anymore, thank God," she said.

"Golightly not ordered you back to work yet?"

155

"Next week," Sadie told him. "I'm still writing up my report. We got the intel on Hank Grayson yesterday. Did you know he was discharged from the US Army for being part of some neo-Nazi militia? He was suspected of far-right terrorism in the past, before he moved back to his hometown and kept his head down. Until he decided to try his hand at ecoterrorism instead. I doubt if he ever really cared about the environment or the local fishing industry. He just thrived on violence and mayhem. The local sheriff found bomb-making materials at his place. Although they didn't blow the rig, I'm sure if I hadn't caught him, he would have planned something else."

Cooper shook his head. "Wow. What a guy. You deserve a medal for taking him down."

There was a brief silence as they both contemplated the alternative.

"So," Cooper said eventually, "I have a half day tomorrow morning. If you're ready, I could pick you up early and we could try and figure out your father's map."

For a moment, Sadie couldn't speak. Now the moment was here, she felt nothing but apprehension.

"Yes," she said after a pause. "Let's do that."

It was time to find out who had killed her sister.

CHAPTER THIRTY

Sadie stared out the window of Logan Cooper's snowcat. It was late morning, and the sun was brighter than usual, illuminating the snow-laden landscape around them.

She had been back in Alaska long enough to have gotten used to its backdrop of frozen tundra, snow-capped mountains, and looming pine forests, but this morning its beauty hit her afresh, taking her breath away.

As they drove toward the pines at the feet of the Chugach Mountains, there was a quiet anticipation in the air between them. Neither of them had spoken much since Cooper had picked her up from the saloon. It was the first time they had been alone since her rescue from the Beaufort, and she still felt embarrassed by her half-delirious confessions of desire for him. Thank God Cooper had the good grace not to mention it, at least so far.

She wasn't entirely sure that was a good thing, though. The fact that he wasn't teasing her mercilessly about it suggested he was thinking about it as hard as she was.

That wasn't the reason Sadie was quiet, though. This was also the first time they had attempted to physically follow the map her father had drawn in his last moments, and there was a swarm of emotions inside her. Hope that she might finally begin to find out the truth about her sister's death.

Dread that what she discovered would be something she would wish she had never known.

And of course, dread that they would find nothing, and that she would be left with the same questions surrounding Jessica's death that she had carried for the last fifteen years.

That she would never find justice for her sister.

Because in her darkest moments, like the long hours of early morning when she had awoken from one of her nightmares, Sadie knew that in many ways, her entire life still pivoted around the moment that Jessica had gone missing. That it had been her sister's murder that had solidified her intention to become a federal agent.

That no matter how many cases she solved, or how many killers she brought to justice, none of it really meant anything to her if she couldn't solve this one.

There was a hope that she only admitted to in those dark hours, too.

That maybe if she could find out what happened to Jessica, the nightmares would stop.

"Sadie, are you okay?"

Cooper's voice jolted her out of her reverie. He didn't use her first name very often.

"I think so," she replied honestly. "It's just...I'm almost scared of what I might find."

There was a shocked silence from Cooper. "Wow," he said eventually.

"Wow?"

"It's not like you to show the slightest chink in your armor," he pointed out. "I've seen you close to death, kidnapped, and naked, and I don't think you have ever gotten that vulnerable with me."

Sadie's head snapped around to glare at him. "You have *not* seen me naked."

A slight grin played around the corners of Cooper's mouth. "There was that case, just before Christmas, when that guy..."

"Just shut up, Cooper," Sadie snapped. Cooper wisely decided to shut up.

She stared down at her father's map, clutched tightly in her hand, trying not to think about Cooper seeing her naked.

"So, what have you got so far?" she said tightly, before he could probe her emotional state any further... or make any more cracks about past cases.

Cooper cleared his throat. "To be honest, not enough. It's definitely this area that he has drawn, I would put money on it. They have to be trees in the top right-hand corner, look, with the Chugach Mountains behind them."

"There are a hell of a lot of trees and mountains around her, though," Sadie said, wondering if Cooper was just seeing what was familiar.

"I know, but see that set of markings near the center? I'm pretty sure that is supposed to be the gorge and the frozen lake next to it."

Sadie tipped her head to one side, trying to see what Cooper was seeing.

"Maybe," she said doubtfully, "but honestly Cooper, it could be anything."

"Well," Cooper acknowledged, "that's why it has been taking so long to figure out. But then I plotted the actual directions with a compass, because for all your father's lack of drawing skills when he did the map, he used to do a lot of hunting and trapping, right?"

Sadie nodded. "Yeah. Before he became a reclusive alcoholic, anyway," she said bitterly. Cooper shot her a sympathetic look.

"Right. So I figured that his sense of direction was probably pretty spot on. Those squiggles and the circle are exactly southeast from the trees and mountains. And if you come out of the main path from the pine forest and go exactly southeast, that's where you get to; the gorge and the lake."

Sadie looked at him as his words gave her a sudden fizz of excitement. "That's brilliant, Cooper!" She was gratified to see a spot of color high on the cheekbones facing her. But he deserved the praise—he must have gone physically trekking around in the snow to figure it out, and the fact that he had gone to that much effort for her was touching.

"Thanks," he said modestly. "The problem, though, is I just can't work out what that little cluster of marks near the X is supposed to be. Especially as they're so smudged. I thought they might be the group of cabins that the seasonal visitors use, but the direction isn't right."

Sadie frowned as she looked at the marks, turning the map to see it from different angles. Cooper was right. It could be the cabins from the way they were clustered together, but one mark was bigger than the others that were fanned around it, and that made no sense. The cabins were pretty uniform.

But then, if her father's faculties had been going rapidly, and his motor skills affected, perhaps his accuracy didn't hold for all parts of the map.

"Well, what happens if you follow the direction exactly?" she asked.

"You end up in the river," Cooper said. "And there's nothing around that resembles the clusters of marks, so it's impossible to work out exactly what the X is pointing to. Unless your father is trying to indicate that we dredge that length of the river, but that still begs the question of the marks. They must be significant. I've checked out the cabin theory, but then there's nothing that could indicate the X. Your father clearly had a very specific spot in mind."

Sadie nodded thoughtfully as she continued turning the map. "Okay, so where is it we're going today?"

"Towards the X. The part of the river it takes you to is up by the headwaters. Where those last bear killings happened. I thought maybe if we look around together, we might figure it out."

Sadie nodded again, hoping Cooper was right. If they couldn't make sense of this and the map turned out to be a dead end, then she was back to square one.

As they drove toward the headwaters, something nagged at the edges of Sadie's mind, trying to get her attention. Something that Cooper had said was significant, but what?

"This is far as I can take the snowcat without getting stuck," Cooper said. "But it's not far to walk to the headwaters."

Sadie didn't reply. She was staring at the map, watching as the penciled cluster marks took on a new shape in front of her eyes.

"Cooper!" she shouted excitedly, making the sheriff nearly jump out of his seat. "I've got it! The clusters. They're not the cabins. Look. It's a bear paw!"

Cooper's eyes widened as he looked down at the map. "Yes, of course it is!" He sounded as excited as she did. "And right near the headwaters are the bears' seasonal feeding grounds. Why didn't I realize?"

"But then, what's the X?" Sadie said. Identifying the exact part of the river didn't necessarily get them anywhere if there was nothing to mark the X.

"The large rock that you can stand on to watch the bears feeding without them seeing you," Cooper said. "Remember the wildlife guy showed us when we were investigating those maneaters?"

Sadie nodded as all the pieces fell into place. "My dad used to go on a lot of bear hunts when we were little," she said. "He would have known the area. So, what do we do, dig around the rock?"

"Let's go and have a look," Cooper said eagerly, reaching for the door handle to let himself out. Sadie laid a hand on his arm.

"Wait," she said softly. Cooper turned to look at her, a quizzical look on his face. "What is it?"

"Thank you," she said quietly. "For everything."

For a long moment, they just stared at each other, and afterwards Sadie never would be able to say who had made the first move. As if drawn together by a magnet, they leaned into each other.

When Cooper's lips brushed hers, Sadie didn't pull away. Instead, her mouth parted under his, and the touch and taste of him sent a warmth rushing through her that she hadn't felt for a very, very long time.

He reached up a hand, burying it in her hair as she slipped an arm around his back, pulling him in closer. Everything about him was familiar, his smell, his build; even the taste of his mouth was exactly what she would have expected. And yet, for all Cooper's familiarity, the sensations were also entirely new and unexpected.

The kiss was brief, but as they gently pulled away from each other Sadie had the sense that somehow, the whole world had changed.

Cooper smiled almost shyly. "I think that deserves another wow." He grinned. Sadie grinned back, for once not fighting the feelings that bubbled up inside her.

Cooper held a hand out toward her. "Shall we?" he said.

As Sadie took his hand and let him help her down from the snowcat, she got the feeling that by taking his hand she had, on some level, said yes to more than getting out of the vehicle and going on a hunt for the location of the X.

For now, though, whatever had just begun between her and Cooper would have to wait.

She had another murder to solve.

NOW AVAILABLE FOR PRE-ORDER!

<u>ONLY SPITE</u>
(A Sadie Price FBI Suspense Thriller—Book 5)

In the endless night of the Alaskan winter, bodies are turning up in the underside of urban Anchorage, wrapped dramatically in plastic. As FBI Special Agent Sadie Price wades through the dark underbelly of the city in her search for answers, she soon realizes this case may just be more disturbing—and shocking—than she thought.

ONLY SPITE (A Sadie Price FBI Suspense Thriller) is book #5 in a chilling new series by mystery and thriller author Rylie Dark, which begins with ONLY MURDER (book #1).

Special Agent Sadie Price, a 29-year-old rising star in the FBI's BAU unit, stuns her colleagues by requesting reassignment to the FBI's remote Alaskan field office. Back in her home state, a place she vowed she would never return, Sadie, running from a secret in her recent past and back into her old one, finds herself facing her demons—including her sister's unsolved murder—while assigned to hunt down a new serial killer.

In the blackness and isolation of the dark season, anyone would lose their mind—which means anyone could be a suspect. But the clock is ticking, and Sadie must track down the killer before he claims another victim—while battling demons re-surfacing from her own dark past.

An action-packed page-turner, the SADIE PRICE series is a riveting crime thriller, jammed with suspense, surprises and twists and turns that you won't see coming. It will have you fall in love with a brilliant and scarred new character, while challenging you, amidst a barren landscape, to solve an impenetrable crime.

Book 6—ONLY MADNESS—is also available.

Rylie Dark

Debut author Rylie Dark is author of the SADIE PRICE FBI SUSPENSE THRILLER series, comprising six books (and counting); the MIA NORTH FBI SUSPENSE THRILLER series, comprising six books (and counting); the CARLY SEE FBI SUSPENSE THRILLER, comprising six books (and counting); and the MORGAN STARK FBI SUSPENSE THRILLER, comprising three books (and counting).

An avid reader and lifelong fan of the mystery and thriller genres, Rylie loves to hear from you, so please feel free to visit www.ryliedark.com to learn more and stay in touch.

BOOKS BY RYLIE DARK

SADIE PRICE FBI SUSPENSE THRILLER
ONLY MURDER (Book #1)
ONLY RAGE (Book #2)
ONLY HIS (Book #3)
ONLY ONCE (Book #4)
ONLY SPITE (Book #5)
ONLY MADNESS (Book #6)

MIA NORTH FBI SUSPENSE THRILLER
SEE HER RUN (Book #1)
SEE HER HIDE (Book #2)
SEE HER SCREAM (Book #3)
SEE HER VANISH (Book #4)
SEE HER GONE (Book #5)
SEE HER DEAD (Book #6)

CARLY SEE FBI SUSPENSE THRILLER
NO WAY OUT (Book #1)
NO WAY BACK (Book #2)
NO WAY HOME (Book #3)
NO WAY LEFT (Book #4)
NO WAY UP (Book #5)
NO WAY TO DIE (Book #6)

MORGAN STARK FBI SUSPENSE THRILLER
TOO LATE (Book #1)
TOO CLOSE (Book #2)
TOO FAR GONE (Book #3)